Tom Flasl

CW00537741

Desert Ghost

Abir Gupta

Nitya Publications

First Edition 2023

All rights reserved

The characters and events portrayed in this book are fictitious. Any similarity to real persons, living or dead, is coincidental and not intended by the author.

No part of this book may be reproduced, or stored in a retrieval system, or transmitted in any form or by any means, electronic, mechanical, photocopying, recording, or otherwise, without express written permission of the publisher.

Copyright © Abir Gupta

ISBN: 978-81-19147-95-3

Published & Printed by:
Nitya Publications, Bhopal MP India
Web: www.nityapublications.com
Email: info@nityapublications.com
Mob: 9009291840

Disclaimer

This book has been published with all reasonable efforts to make the material error-free after the author's consent. No part of this book shall be used or reproduced in any manner. The author of this book is solely responsible and liable for its content, including but not limited to the views, representations, descriptions, statements, information, opinions, and references ["Content"].

It is not endorsed, authorized, licensed, sponsored, or supported by any other entity owning or controlling right to the any other name, trademarks or copyrights.

The Content of this book shall not constitute or be construed or deemed to reflect the opinion or expression of the Publisher or Editor.

This book is sold subject to the condition that it shall not, by way of trade or otherwise, be lent, resold, reprint, re-distribute, hired out, or otherwise circulated, without the publisher's prior consent, in any form of binding or cover other than that it is originally published.

Abir Gupta

Have Fun Reading.

Contents

Chapter 1

There was no wind. The icy winter air hung still. The deafening silence rang throughout Tom's ears. A carefree robin traversed the skies, invisible to him. He pulled back the string, slightly adjusting his stance. Tom's senses were on key as the bow's cord went taut. The arrow's tip bore its piercing gaze into the target. Everything surrounding the boy and bow were in a long-forgotten dream. The soiled dummy thirty meters in front of Tom, with its empty eyes and wicked smile etched on its face seemed to be mocking him.

Every ounce of Tom's concentration was centred between its ghostly eyes. "Without forgetting the world around you, training your mind to focus at the target, you will not succeed." His father's words echoed around him. Tom forced the diversion away. He needed to concentrate. The boy's lungs were already aching. This was his chance. He let go of the string.

Tom momentarily felt it rub against his leather arm-pad as the arrow whistled through the air. It was unstoppable. Tom released his breath as the deadly point penetrated into the scarecrow. He watched as a flurry of straw showered itself onto the frosted grass. The target fell to the ground as the light breeze, creating patterns on the grass, blew its remains across the spatial backyard.

It had just started to snow and Tom brushed the dainty flakes off his ruggedly handsome dirty blonde hair for a fourteen-year-old boy. The snow had significantly intensified in the unstable weather pattern of England but that didn't bother Tom. He set his training bow on the ground and unhooked his arm-pad, relaxing his muscles. He walked towards the target, somewhat nervous. His boots crunched loudly on the syrupy, wafer-thin layer of ice coating the floor, making him dream of the comfortably balmy air of a late Autumn's evening in North Africa, the aromatic smell of spices hanging in the sky...

Tom turned over the target which had already been covered in a smattering of snow. It was a heap of rags; the many years of practice had shredded it to ruins bit by bit. It was identical to the weather beaten scarecrows timidly populating the ramshackle countryside farms haphazardly situated all throughout England.

Tom often found it hard to believe that the boiled carrots on his plate on a Sunday afternoon, dripping with gravy, had started their long journey at a place like that. He critically examined the scarecrow. There was a number of slits on the back of its head, expertly done by his father through the eye sockets. Tom's father was an elitist at weapons such as the bow and never failed to disappoint the audience.

It always bought dismay whenever he saw them. Tom had never considered himself ranked above his father. The bow, he declared, was apparently his weakness in the array of deadly weapons he could wield with such finesse. Yet, the back of the mannequin's head was peppered with so many holes that there would soon be none of it left. He was also brusquely reminded of the time when he had, out of boredom, invited a few of his friends over at his house.

Tom had been younger then, thinking he was superior over his peers because he was, according to himself, a crack shot at the ancient weapon. Across four of his friends, he had made a laughing stock of himself.

Evidence of that was the crude scar under the targets armpit. The arrow tip, he remembered clearly, grazed its side and flew into a particularly nasty thorn bush. It wasn't a terrible shot for a regular nine-year-old child but boasting about a headshot scored thirty meters away, his current target, didn't help.

Tom brushed off the dried hay, looking for the mark in the forehead. It wasn't there. He had failed. Tom's heart dropped as he saw the fibreglass shaft protruded a few centimetres left of the nose (a dirt-encrusted button from his smart tuxedo, now many sizes too small for him). His parents were prepared to turn a one hundred and sixty pound suit into spare parts for a training dummy so their son could master the bow.

Tom irately wrenched the arrow out of the targets face and froze as he heard boots thumping across the cobbled patio. It was his father. Jacob Flashfire was an imposing man, well built with the same shabby yet striking haircut as his only son. He was wearing a casual yet expensive sheepskin leather jacket. It was paired along with his custom-made designer denim jeans. On top of that, Tom's affluent father sported a pair of exclusive Doctor Martens. The pair of well-lubricated boots announced the man's arrival with a heavy thud, adding to his impressive stature. And his eyes. They were like the ocean. Sparkling, green water most of the time but could easily turn into a tempestuous storm if he was irritated. This feature he had also passed on to Tom. He was like a miniature model of Jacob.

He looked so at ease, yet always vigilant. If anything even slightly suspicious occurred, Jacob Flashfire was there, on the balls of his feet with his senses keyed up to the max. Whether he was flipping burger patties on the barbeque, or dishing out cards between his friends at a party, he was always ready.

But his explanation for the family's immense wealth was because he was the manager of a thriving company which manufactured plane turbines. Tom was immediately suspicious of that statement remembering when his dad had returned after a week's business trip. He had returned with the usual presents and foreign chocolates, but also with a malicious selection of cuts and bruises. There had always been something off about his father. And Tom was about to find out soon.

Tom didn't understand how working as a big company manager could be a precarious job. He had come to the conclusion of an accident while inspecting a helicopter rotor. But still...

"Tut, tut, Tom." Jacob approached his son and seizing the dummy from him. He held the shredded potato sack up to the sky. The sun glinted through the blanket of sombre clouds. A typical English winter. Tom heard his dad sigh disapprovingly. "It's barely pierced the skin of the bag! And that too on the cheek! You'll have trouble against the pheasants in Battleberry Hill! Listen, Tom. You're a Flashfire. It's in your blood. When I was your age, I could..."

Tom growled under his breath. Couldn't anything he did be good enough for his dad? Anyways, he had long ago decided that he hated pheasant-hunting.

Tom was lost lamenting to himself while his dad tried to get his attention. "Tom? Tom? Are you listening?"

He looked up. "Sorry?" Tom had the habit of daydreaming much to the dislike of his father, who honestly reminded him of a strict substitute mathematics teacher who scolded him whenever he got the gradient of an arrow shot incorrect.

"Listen, I'm going away on another business trip. There's some food left for you in the fridge and you know how to work the microwave. I should be back in a few day's time. See you." Tom secretly exploded with ecstasy. A few days of undisturbed gaming time after school and then the Christmas holidays. Microwave meals, a 65-inch plasma TV, a larder of his favourite snacks and his assortment of video games. That was all he needed. It had been a while since he had a few days just to himself doing nothing.

He kept the excitement for later and asked, "Will Mum be home?" Tom's mother worked as an Orthopaedic Surgeon in Maidenhead and her schedule was always full, even on the weekends. Tom barely saw her: she came home at twelve, and by then Tom was asleep. On the weekends, even later. Tom wondered how she managed to do it. His parent's hectic jobs were the reason for their stately home and riches but sometimes Tom wondered if things weren't exactly as they seemed...

Chapter 2

The mahogany grandfather clock chime six, collecting dust in the Flashfire's palatial living room. While the furniture and rugs were pricey, the house had an old fashioned feel to it, something that didn't belong in Central London with its cramped houses and driveways chocked with dull Toyotas and people every few feet, their noses a few inches away from a screen.

The Cinnamon Grove House wasn't considered a mansion by either passer-bys or locals, but still the biggest house in the area by a substantial amount. The rest of the London houses were jammed together in jumbled rows with wild bushes engulfing them. The Cinnamon Grove was the exact inverse.

It was surrounded by a hedgerow incongruous amongst the untamed greenery. It was somewhat distant from the rest of the houses, quietly sitting a few blocks away from the chaos of real London. The cobbled courtyard and ivy draped around the side of the house reminded many of peaceful seaside cottage.

Tom sat on the dining table completing a English essay. He had never been the best at studies but English had always been his forte. Tom sat on the comfortable black leather dining chair which surrounded the extendable Agar wood table. It could seat eight people, twelve when extended.

Sadly, it was never full as most of Tom's relatives apart from his parents and mum's parents lived in America. Suddenly, a powerful gust of wind blew into the living room through the open windows. It was accompanied by the drone of helicopter rotors which Tom hadn't noticed earlier because he was so engrossed in his essay.

He heard the heavy stomping of feet on the carpeted stairs as his dad arrived downstairs. Tom jumped of his chair and went to greet him. Jacob Flashfire was wearing one of his smartest tuxes, grey with a pink-and-black tie, which had somehow avoided being turned into a dummy's nose. Yet, instead of a briefcase for his files, Tom's dad had an adventurer rucksack. It was something that people looking to conquer the jungle or desert would carry.

He briefly acknowledged his son with a nod and a smile, turned to the door. But as he did so, Tom noticed something poking out of a black leather pouch attached to the man's belt. But then Jacob stepped out through the double door entrance before Tom could see what it was.

Tom tried to follow his dad outside but stopped when he saw the helicopter. The first thing he noticed was its vast size. It took up most of the front yard, dwarfing the naive buttercups lined up in the soil. The dangerous rotors were precariously close to Jacob's elegant topiaries, something he wasn't happy about.

It was a beautiful Sikorsky UH-60 Black Hawk. It was painted Camouflage, the dark greens and browns blending together in twisting patterns. It had four razor helicopter blades and a twin engine. It was truly a masterpiece of modern engineering. The chopper was typically used by the American Army for air assaults, aero medical evacuations and for transport. Tom also observed, placed on the belly of the helicopter, a laser-designated-air-to-ground-missile.

This was becoming increasingly doubtful. Why had an armed helicopter appeared out of the blue to take his father abroad to do business? And Tom was almost sure about the object he had seen his father carrying. But it couldn't have been! Tom watched his father enter the vehicle, saluting the pilot. He was a gruff, pot-bellied man who should have been pensioned off years ago.

Jacob smiled at his son one last time before disappearing into the interior of the Blackhawk.

Tom frowned before slamming the front door shut to shield himself from the airstream. He briefly wondered what the Londoners would think as they saw an army helicopter flying above their heads.

Tom then returned to the dining table and shut his book. His dad had told him that his mother wouldn't be coming home as her agenda was full (as always). Tom comforted himself by heading to the fridge and took out a tub of cookie dough ice cream.

He flopped down on the couch, ripping off the plastic covers that were there to ensure the expensive leather didn't get damaged. He grabbed the TV remote and continued the series he was watching. A perfect day for a teenage boy.

***

The man's voice crackled over the intercom. "We're in range. Go!" The Blackhawk soared through the stifling curtain of heat, the merciless sun beating down on it as if forcing it away. The metal doors slid open, sending a hot blast of air into Jacob's face. It was a hurricane inside the metal box. Jacob had changed into a few thin layers of clothing that would ventilate the desert air. He gulped. Everything was ready. The parachute double-checked, plenty of food and water, supplies, a map.

Nevertheless, he hadn't been this nervous in his life. For what he was heading towards was even more lethal than the barren sea of sand below him. But there was no going back now. It was for the safety of what was quite possible the whole world. He took one last look at the appealing, air-conditioned hold. He could do this. Jacob took one deep breath and jumped.

Chapter 3

The fourteen-year old looked with distaste at the forest-green blazer, freshly ironed, along with the charcoal-grey trousers. He couldn't think of a more mind-numbing colour choice for a school uniform. Sluggishly he did up his lime-striped blue tie in front of his mirrored wardrobe. It was seven in the morning and Tom hopeful for the last day of term before the Christmas holidays.

Tom admired his intense green eyes and dirty blonde hair, shabbily thrown around on the top of his head. He was physically in wonderful shape, one of those blessed people who could gobble limitlessly and still remain a similar size. Already, there was firm muscles were developing underneath his grey sweater. Tom took one last look at himself and headed for the door.

Tom went to St. Mary's, a secondary Comprehensive school. He expected his dad to send him to a private or boarding school, but protested and was instead permitted to go to St. Mary's where the majority of his friends were planning to go. Tom had felt he wouldn't fit in at a posh school abroad and wasn't going to trade friends for learning how to knot a bow tie.

Tom walked out of the house into the dreary, hopeless morning, the time of year little children prayed for snow but their wish was never fulfilled. Tom trudged through the whirl of raindrops engulfing him and watched as little children carrying princess umbrellas crossed the street. It was all so... boring. Tom sometimes wondered if it was really that necessary to attend school five days a week. Would it really help him become a professional footballer?

Even as he pondered, the red brick building was growing ever closer and the stream of students entering through the corrugated iron gates became a mass of bobbing heads as they were let into the building. The familiar main school building was surrounded by a separate sixth-form block, contrasting modern black tiles and tinted windows creating an austere office tone. Tom was joined by his best friend Harrison or 'Harris' Parker, a boy Tom had met on his first day at St Mary's. He had brown hair and originated from Brazil. Together they entered through the side doorway for another day of school.

***

Tom's elbow slid across the table surface as he dozed through the lesson. His lab partner, a girl with dark hair and perfect grades called Laura edged away from him. Biology was Tom's least favourite subject, learning about GM crops and dissecting animals. It was an engrossing subject for some but the information just went in one ear and out the other. Then suddenly, the class's pitiless teacher barked, "TOM! Are you listening? Now, what was the scientific term for a yellow fat-tailed scorpion?"

Tom was stupefied. "Wha- Oh, Andro-whatnot..." He had barely been listening in his half-awake, half-asleep state. The class laughed. Mr Porryfield sighed. "That's detention, four o'clock. You weren't paying any attention, Tom. The correct term is Androctonus australis. It is one of the most venomous scorpions in the world, nearly as lethal as the cobra. The species inhabit the deserts spanning across North Africa. It averages at ten centimetres of length and its stings, in most cases, lead to death. Thank you for your help."

The class sniggered once more. Tom sighed and rested his head on the table, listening as Mr Porryfield rambled about spiders and snakes. He was capable of channelling his concentration into a bow, worthy enough of making fairly excellent shots but not into Andro-whatnots, or whatever they were called. Tom anticipated for the moment where the divine bell would liberate him from the Biology class. A sound started resonating throughout the school building. The bell brought with it the howls of teenagers as they stampeded out of the class. Tom turned to leave with his friends before he heard somebody call his name softly. It was Mr Porryfield.

His shining, smart shoes squeaked across the floor as he waited for the last student to exit. He then shut the door and said, "We need to talk." Tom groaned inwardly. Wasn't a detention enough? That was every schoolchild's least favourite phrase. Tom felt the desperate urge to run away, felling awkward alone with his teacher. But the last thing he needed a day before the holidays was a double detention. Reluctantly he turned around and spoke in his most polite voice. "Yes?"

"Take a seat." Tom thought Mr Porryfield was being peculiarly friendly, though he noticed a strain to his voice. He was obviously trying to not snap at the ignorant student in front of him. He dragged a stool out from under an old wooden table, embedded with acid burns, pencil drawings and other specks of scientific damage. Tom swung his bag of his shoulder and sat down, face to face with his teacher. With Mr Porryfield's collared shirt and old-fashioned bow tie, Tom felt like he was attending his grandfather's eightieth birthday party.

Tom also wondered if this was how he dressed out of school. He was only young, around twenty-five and with his calculator in his breast pocket, Tom thought he was better suited as an accountant.

"Thank you. Now, I want to talk about the episode in our lesson today. Tom, I know the GSCE's aren't going to be easy, and you can't afford to doze off in lessons. Biology can open up many career paths for you and I'd be disappointed to see you miss the pass mark. Look, you're a smart kid. I saw your mock results. All you have to do is pay more attention, have a more open mindset and you will succeed. By the way, there's no detention. It's the Christmas holidays so I thought I shouldn't ruin the spirit."

Tom murmured a thanks and showed himself out. "Oh, and Tom? One more thing," Tom twisted round to listen. "You never know but the things you've learned today, in this school, may one day be of use to you!" He winked at Tom.

Tom grinned and ran out of the classroom. He was free! "Tom! No running in the corridor!" Tom just smiled.

Chapter 4

The man had already pushed himself beyond the limit. He was utterly exhausted and was on the verge of running out of supplies. And he had found no information about his target. The blistering sun, the endless dunes, it was all too much. Jacob had reached the end.

"Marge?" the man spoke the name with a demanding tone in his voice. He was well-built but aging fast, grey wisps of hair appearing in the jet-black mess usually cut short. He wore casual jeans and a polo shirt that was stretched against his muscle. He was only thirty-seven years old but his time at ISSO had turned him harder, more aloof from the rest of the world. His name was Jonathan Turner. He was the head of ISIO- Intelligence, Spy, Information, Operation.

"Hmm?"

There was a middle-age African woman staring at the computer with a frown on her face. She wore a knitted cardigan and had quadrangle spectacles. She looked up from her work. "Any sign of him?"

Miss Challaby sighed. "No. It seems like they removed his tracker. We have absolutely no idea where he is." She looked down sadly. Jonathan Turner paced the room, thinking hard with his critical mind. "Not good, not good." he muttered.

"Dispatch A, B, C and D squad. That's sixteen experienced men searching the Sahara. Also, prepare the Bell 212 and Watchkeeper. "

He was referring to UK military helicopters which ISIO owned. "Keep reserve Unit 1 on alert. He's our best man. We can't afford to lose him. Do whatever you can to find him."Miss Challaby frowned. "Do you think that is enough men? I mean, the Sahara Desert is nearly the size of the USA! I've been there myself. Jacob might not have long left."

The head of the secret operation rubbed his chin and stared outside the frosted windows. He sipped on his Cappuccino while he contemplated on the various solutions before coming to a decision. "Send them all."

***

The silver moon rose above the dying sun in the twilight. Tom was slouched out on the couch on his Nintendo Switch. He boosted his car forward and smashed into the large ball. It rolled of the wall and Tom jumped up, smashing the football into the goal. He smiled as he was thrown backwards and watched the epic replay. Rocket League was one of his favourite video games for a Saturday night. Tom loved football and supported Arsenal. Getting slightly bored after winning the sixth match in a row, Tom threw his Nintendo on the sofa and casually flicked through the newspaper sitting on the side table.

There was the usual adverts and interviews but then:

SMUGGLERS ACROSS AFRICA!

We have been informed by a secret source that Smugglers are active across the African Continent. These are very dangerous people and it is suspected that they are heading to Morocco over the Sahara Desert. It is unknown currently what they are smuggling but either way it is suspected to be illegal items and authorities are trying to stop them at every cost.

It is likely that the smuggler come from African Countries further South, from countries like Ghana and Nigeria. Smugglers like these pollute whole continents with their greed, most commonly in Asia and Africa. Authorities are on high alert as shipments come into the UK.

Tom yawned and put down the newspaper. He had already eaten his supper and was fatigued, even though he had done nothing all day. The short entry continued down the page but Tom was going to bed. He slipped on his pyjamas, brushed his teeth, then sank into the comfort of his luxurious king-sized bed. He drew the blue curtains and fell soundly asleep.

Knock, knock. Tom uncomfortably turned in his sleep. Knock, knock. The sound had barely penetrated through the shut door. Knock, knock. It was getting louder. Tom groaned and stretched his arms, accidentally knocking his knuckles into the light switch. "Aargh!" Tom squeezed his eyes shut, blinded. KNOCK, KNOCK!

The sound was crisp in the silence of- Tom checked his phone lying on the drawer beside the bed- 3 A.M.! Who was at his house at this time of the night? Tom started to feel a little apprehensive. He was alone in the house and the police would take too long to arrive at his house. But what if it was just his imagination?

Tom cantankerously clambered out of his bed and hurried to the en-suite bathroom. He splashed his face with water and looked in the mirror. His hair was a rat's nest and there were bags under his sea- green eyes. Tom stumbled down the stairs. Were they still there? Suddenly, BANG!

It was like someone had thumped on the door with a sledge hammer. Tom was very scared now. He lingered at the bottom step, afraid. He crept up and stared at the door. Wouldn't somebody hear? But house was surrounded by hedges- they would have absorbed all the sound. The thumping continued this time with a rush of angry words, inaudible but very loud. Tom couldn't open that door. Instead, he left the hallway and tiptoed to the window.

Tom craned his neck to the side as he tried to catch a glimpse of the man- he had heard him speak. It was presumably only one person, which was a relief. What could they want from him? He saw a tall, stocky man through the glass but it was too dark to make out any of his features. Then, in the moment Tom was completely visible to the man, he turned around and stared at him through the window. Tom immediately ducked down but realised he had no fear- the glass was frosted. Tom was hidden. He sighed with relief but butterflies were still fluttering around in his stomach.

It was silent. Tom returned to the door, wary. Had he gone! Then came the unexpected. There was a hideous sound as sharp metal came poking out of the door. Splinters of wood flew everywhere and Tom hurled himself to the floor. He couldn't believe it. It was... a knife!

Tom shivered. He was in grave danger. Then, mercifully, Tom heard the sound of footsteps. It were diminishing away into the distance, taking with it the horrifying memory of that night. Tom nearly laughed with joy. Startlingly, Tom felt a hot tear trickle down his cheek. He felt angry with himself. He brushed it away with his shirt sleeve. It was nothing. But Tom wasn't so sure as he looked at the lethal knife staring at him with one cold eye.

It wasn't over yet.

Chapter 5

Tom awoke late that morning, mere hours after the incident earlier that night. He had scurried up the stairs and hid himself, wrapped in the protective arms of the duvet. He felt horrible, like waking up on a Monday morning for school.

After Tom woke up, he lay in bed, replaying the night's dreadful ordeal. He rolled up his curtains as the sunlight pierced through the window, painfully reminding Tom of the knife. The knife. Was it still there? Without brushing his teeth, Tom stampeded down the stairs.

And, sure enough, it was still there, as menacing as ever. Tom boldly walked over to the door. The attacker had left. He was sure of it. The carpet placed at the door was showered in splinters. Tom twisted open the lock and stepped outside. He shivered in the winter's bitter cold.

It was a beautiful day and the sun was out, but ineffective against the breeze blowing across London. Dew had gathered on the prim grass and Tom heard the thunderous sound of cars during the rush hour, still busy in the holidays. Also, it had rained last night, washing the air clean but at the same time possibly washing away traces of the man.

Tom scrutinized the door on the outside. The weapon was a regular kitchen knife with a black rubber handle but around fifteen centimetres long. It was deeply lodged into the door, telling Tom the man meant business. He grabbed the handle and pulled as hard as he could. It didn't come out. He tried again and the second time it came free. Tom stumbled backwards, knife in hand.

A grouchy tabby cat was spread out on the lawn. It squealed and darted away at incredible speed. So these were no small-time criminals. The man had wanted something from Tom and the worst part was that Tom had no idea why he was endangered.

Last night, Tom wasn't able to make out the man's characteristics. However, there was somewhere he knew he could look. Tom shut the front door and put the knife on the countertop. He hurried upstairs and entered the Cinnamon Grove's library.

It wasn't very big, just the size of a regular living room. The leather-bound books defined the room, hinting the wealth of the Flashfires. Tom left damp footprints from his bare feet on the spongy red carpet. There were hundreds of books crammed together on the towering shelves, overwhelming Tom. While he liked reading, he rarely entered the library as most of the books were in Latin.

But that wasn't what he was after. On a circular, metal table coated in wooden paint, there was a computer. This room was often used by Jacob Flashfire as an office, as he enjoyed the peace and quiet. Tom powered on the computer and typed in the password which he knew off by heart. With access to his father's laptop, he could view the CCTV recordings.

He would upload them onto a USB stick then, along with the knife, head over to the police station. It seemed like the best thing to do because the attacker could strike again at any time. Tom pressed down on a key and viewed the recordings. There were a grand total of three cameras associated with the Cinnamon Grove. Two watching over the front door, and one recording the happenings in the expansive gardens.

Tom checked the first one, for the garden. There was nothing unusual on the screen so Tom tried to check the other two. Nothing. The screen was blank. That was odd. It looked as if they had jammed or been sabotaged.

He shut down the device and went back out onto the porch. He slipped on his boots and stepped off the path. One of the High-Tech cameras was hidden amongst the hedges, invisible to anyone who tried to enter the house but it had a perfect view of the gate. Tom wrenched it out of the bushes and winced as a sharp thorn dug into him.

He pulled out the camera, removing the wire. Tom gasped. The glass had been shattered. A loose wire from the circuitry hung out, sparking. Tom held the camera upside down and something fell out from the circuitry.

It was a small metal object. Tom nudged it with his toe before recognizing it. It was a bullet. Tom stared at it with disbelief, then ran to the garden shed and put on a pair of grubby gloves as a precaution. He returned to the porch and picked up the bullet. It looked so small but in reality it was part of the most deadly thing a man could carry.

It was similar to a Full Metal Jacket, used mainly for pistols. Strangely, Tom hadn't heard the shot. The man must have used a silencer.

Tom trembled. This had just got a lot more complicated. What was the man's reason to shoot out the cameras? Was what he was doing really that bad? Tom slipped the bullet into his pocket. This needed serious attention. His boot's crunched on the cobbled steps which were glinting with shards of glass. The next camera was less obscure then the first, clearly detectable above the window.

Unsurprisingly, the ledge was showered with more glass. Another bullet was lying on the grass, damp from the dew. It was identical to the last. Another piece of evidence. Maybe the police could analyse the bullets and find out where they came from. That was all there was to see as the rain had cleansed the path. There were no footprints. He had been there. Then he was gone.

Tom wasn't feeling scared anymore. He was suspicious, angry at the man. This had become a mystery. Was an undisturbed Christmas too much to ask for?

Tom hurried back inside and ran upstairs. He pulled out a metal tin from under his bed and dropped the knife and bullet into it. Along with that, he placed one of the cameras into the box. He would take that to the police later that day. But he really needed a break. With all his homework done, Tom headed out of the house for a walk. He hoped it would clear his mind a little. The man would be arrested and that was that. Hopefully.

Chapter 6

It was so cold. Why was it like this? Unbearably hot in the day but a bone-rattling chill to even things out in the night. Couldn't it ever be...normal?

Jacob needed rest. He had been told it would be cold in the desert but this was on another scale. It was eerily silent, his only company the stars above. The moon illuminated the trickster dunes. With every step Jacob took on one, he seemed to be going backwards. The loose sand just couldn't hold his weight. He was also in dire needed of water. He only had quarter a bottle left, the amount of water that filled a shoe. And he still hadn't found them yet. He wanted out.

On cue, something flashed hundreds of kilometres above him. It was a commercial plane. Jacob seethed with rage. There was heating aboard, meals, reclining seats, air hostesses there to fulfil every wish. Jacob imagined himself smugly watching a movie in his business class compartment, flying above the desert with a glass of icy Cherry Coke in his hands.

He straightened himself up with a new-found motivation. Jacob could complete this mission. He would have to. He had a loving son and wife to return to. Jacob couldn't let his family down. Also, he knew the fridge in the kitchen could have supplied all of London with Cherry Coke. He continued walking.

That was when he saw them.

Tom continued walking down Baker Street. He felt much, much better after his walk. Tom was more relaxed, fresh.

He smiled as a wary squirrel stared at him before scaling a large Sycamore tree like an acrobat. He was holding a nut and began to crack it open, its back to Tom. It was as if he was scared the strange giant beneath him would try and steal its hard-earned nut.

Tom turned the corner down towards his house. He had decided to head straight for the police station, put forward the evidence that relax for the rest of the holidays until his father returned from his "business trip". But the moment Tom arrived at the imposing gates of the Cinnamon Grove he knew that was impossible.

Something had gone very wrong.

Tom could simply tell that by looking at the mud-spattered footprints leading up to the front door. The man had been back. But this time, there were several other, smaller prints accompanying the first. There was more than one this time. The patio was still covered in glass from the earlier.

Tom immediately adapted a fighting stance with his legs apart and fists raised. He was a black belt in taekwondo and he knew more than enough to handle himself in a fight. Tom cautiously approached the front door. It had really put the mood off.

Tom's suspicions were confirmed. It couldn't have been the postman. The front door was ajar and the handle, along with the keyhole was missing. The whole thing had been blown apart. A small section of the door where the handle and keyhole was supposed to be was charred black. To back up the evidence, the floor was littered with bolts and fragments of gold-coated metal.

To Tom, it seemed like a peculiar way of breaking into a house. But it just proved how dangerous those people where. Tom had thought to immediately call the police after what he saw. Suddenly, he realised his phone had been left to charge in his room. He would have to deal with it himself.

Tom nudged the door further open. It creaked and Tom winced. Nothing. He breathed out and headed in. It was still silent. Tom could almost hear his heart pounding louder and louder, trying to escape his ribcage. So far, the only clue that the intruders had invaded were the footprints which Tom decided to follow upstairs.

The prints led into his room first. Tom hesitated, before pushing the doors open and charging in. He relaxed when he saw nobody. Still, it was clear that his room had been searched. The sheets were ruffled, things moved around from where he had last seen them, his cupboards open...

And the metal box. It was still there. Tom had, for some reason, left it buried far back into his cupboard. With a surge of relief he pulled it out and undid the clips. Everything was still in there, including the knife. The knife! Tom picked it up and shut the box. It felt light in his hand, comfortable. By now, he had realised Martial Arts couldn't stop these men, let alone defend him. The knife was the only other way. Of course, Tom knew he would never actually use it unless he was in life-threatening danger. But he felt safe with it in his hands, secure.

There was nothing else to see in his room full of gaming discs, posters and study table piling up with textbooks. Tom took one last look before continuing on the trail of footsteps which seemed to be fading with each step. They led into the other rooms of the Cinnamon Grove but nothing seemed to be missing or unusual. Tom climbed each flight of stairs with the same result. Were they even in the house?

Tom, annoyed at finding nothing trekked up the last few stairs before coming to a stop in front of Jacob Flashfire's office. There had always been something unusual about it. While his dad primarily worked in the quiet library, he occasionally disappeared into his second office. Tom had never been there before- it was out of bounds. Tom could only imagine what secrets it held behind the heavy metal door. It was locked behind an eight-digit combination code, impossible to guess.

Tom had no clue what was in there. Well, it was obviously something important if it had such high, unnecessary, security. Who would try to break in anyway? Someone just had. Tom stared at the door for a few seconds, decorated with cartoon stickers Tom had owned when he was little. Then he noticed the hole.

It was barely big enough for a man to fit it, but possible. There was a perfect circle in the middle of the door, looking as if an electric saw had been involved. They could be in there. Tom, excited, poked his head into the room. Despite everything, he couldn't wait to see what the room on the other side looked like after waiting for fourteen long years.

At first, Tom was surprised. The room was cosy and warm, contradicting the uninviting, cold door blocking it. It had a Persian rug, with a table on top. There were a few framed photos dotted on the walls which were covered in a glittery wallpaper, seeming irrelevant to Tom's father's taste.

Tom climbed in to the room and examined it further. Whatever was in here was clearly important to the men, if they hadn't already found it and left. The photos he realised, were taken of him and his mother. He was younger in the photos, chubby with baby fat and staring at another child who had passed by. His mother was there to, smiling with perfect teeth and red hair.

There was a large table in the middle of the room with a high-tech computer and monitor on top. Tom tried to access it, but it was password protected with another eight-digit code. And that was to open the case where it was held. And Tom suspected trying to blow it up wouldn't help much.

Apart from that, there was nothing. Is that what they wanted? The computer? Tom shook his head and turned around, at the same time knocking a snowball of the Eiffel Tower, bought in Paris, down onto the floor. It smashed and Tom watched with horror as the water soaked into the carpet. The little Eiffel Tower was nestled in the carpet, broken. Had he been heard?

Then came the footsteps.

Tom instinctively dived behind a smaller table covered in a cherry-red table cloth. There was a china plate with scraps of food left on it, that hadn't cleared away. They must have been searching the garden when Tom came into the Cinnamon Grove. He drew the table cloth a little further down, almost completely concealing him. His heart was thumping as he heard the sound downstairs growing louder. They were coming.

He had just made it in time. From the side of the curtain, Tom saw a pair of large feet, wearing loafers. They were followed by another person wearing trainers and black jeans. "What was that?!" the first man snarled. Tom dared to take a closer look and saw that he was tall, well over six feet and African. The second was shorter and spoke with a European accent. He had glasses and wore a bowler hat.

"It was nothing. We already checked this room. C'mon!" The second man replied. The first didn't move. "I smell it. Someone has been here." The man was definitely the one who had tried to break in his way in to the house- he was terrifying. His eyes were filled with fury and perhaps a sliver of fear. "But in the email he sent us it said the papers were here! You illiterate man! Didn't you read the instructions? You call yourself a smuggler but you can't steal as simple piece of paper!" he bellowed.

The second man shivered. "We'll just have to tell him we didn't find them." The African man looked like he was about to punch the European. But then he sighed. "Fine!

Now move!" He shoved the other man out of the way and stomped down the stairs.

Tom shivered. That short encounter had caused him to break into a cold sweat. The knife was still in his hand but he hadn't used it. Tom let it slide out of his hand. He sighed with relief. But the men weren't gone yet. So Tom lay there for another hour before finally crawling, a considerable amount of time after he had heard the door slam shut.

There was plenty space under the table but his muscles still ached. Tom stretched them to get the blood flowing back. Now he could finally think properly. The men had mentioned two words that meant something to Tom: papers and smuggler.

Having just recently read the smuggling paper, he knew that the men were up to no good. As for the papers, Tom had no idea what sort of documents they were looking for. Maybe he would have a look for himself. But if the men couldn't find it, then he probably couldn't. Or 'he' had given the pair the wrong location.

Tom sighed and leant his hand on the wall. Then he felt it moving. "Waah!" Two sections of the wall paper began turning inwards. Tom stabilized himself before peering through the flip door. Wow! It was so well hidden. No wonder the smugglers hadn't found it. Who would have know a clandestine compartment was hidden in the walls?

Tom crawled under the gap into the tiny room. It was no more than the size of a broom shed. There was a small table, the only thing that counted as furniture in the room.

There was also a ladder leading up to a locked trapdoor. But Tom had no need to go there. He knew it led into the attic. Where else?

The thing that interested him were the documents on the table. They were fairly new and no dust had began to settle on them. Tom picked one up and read: DESERT GHOST Drone footage caught of Smuggler moving North-West. Carrying: Unknown." That was all the first page said. There was an illegible signature at the bottom and a date. It was only from a few weeks ago.

So these were the papers. It seemed like a collection of evidence on the smugglers. Suddenly, everything seemed to be coming together. The smugglers had tried to break in to find the papers, which held evidence against them and could get them jailed for the rest of their lives. But why was the evidence here?

Tom got the feeling that his enigmatic father was involved in this mess. He frowned. The files had mentioned a drone footage. Maybe it was somewhere in this room...Tom's first instinct was to look under the floorboards. They wouldn't budge. He felt the walls, searching for more hidden areas. Nothing. But as he was under the table searching, he saw something taped onto the underbelly of the table.

He couldn't see in the gloom but wrenched the object off the table, along with a mass of tape. He ripped of the tape to find himself holding a CD disc. This was the drone footage! This evidence would take down the smugglers in court!

Tom excitedly ran back downstairs into his room. The holidays had already proven to be more interesting than he imagined. Sitting on the top of Tom's shelves was his Xbox. It was already connected to the TV in front of his bed. He slotted in the disc, removing the video game he had been playing and putting it back into its case. He grabbed the controller and waited for it to start.

Chapter 7

The screen flickered into life. It had worked! Tom kept intently watching. Then burst an array of colour on the screen. The first thing Tom noticed was sand. Sand. It was an endless sea of sand.

Tom had been to the beach many times but had never seen the quantity of sand that he was seeing now. He had a bird's eye view of what appeared to be a desert. The sand rippled far into the distance, nothing in sight. No trees. No plants. No life.

The footage had presumably been taken from a drone. Tom heard a faint whirring in the background as something plodded up a dune. Tom gasped. It was a camel. It had two bony humps protruding from its muscled, downy body. Tom thought it looked bizarre: its hairy chin, the swishing tail...

But the drone wasn't interested in the majestic creature. It soared on at a high speed and soon the camel was forgotten miles away. Tom caught a glimpse of the perfect, blue sky, looking as if an passionate artist had poured down a tin of blue paint on a sheet of paper. The whole landscape was perfect.

The drone continued. Tom spotted a bird flying to its left- and eagle. Maybe it thought the drone was prey. But then it lost interest in the strange, metal bird and glided away into the scorching sun, dominating the Sahara.

Soon the drone came across a flat, barren landscape devoid of sand. Salt pans. Hundreds of meters below, there was dark smoke trail rising higher by the minute. The drone was onto something. It descended into the smoke, and for a few seconds the screen went black.

The drone managed to zoom into the scene. Something was going on. Tom saw people, wearing tunics and face wrappings to shield themselves from the sun. The drone kept its distance but Tom could make out a large green tent spread out onto the floor. Around five men were putting it up.
Parked next to the dirty green sheet, amongst the pegs was a dusty Landrover. The wheels were grimy with sand and the paint was chipping off the vehicle. The seats were frayed and fluff was trailing from them. The battered steering wheel was wooden and wires were coiling around each other, dangling from the dashboard.

The car was in awful shape. Loaded into the back, was a crate. Looking around, Tom saw many other men lifting crates around the campsite. Their features were undistinguishable but the number plate of the battered car was clearly visible. On the crates, there was an emblem painted. It was a picture of a snake with a gold coin for its eye. It looked innocent enough. Underneath the symbol were the words DESERT GHOST.

It was a footage of the smugglers. Tom understood the importance of the disc inside his console. The drone zoomed in on one of the man's faces, brown eyes and short, curly hair falling from his mask. The man stood there, panting after moving another crate into a pickup truck Tom hadn't spotted before.

The man took a swig of water from a leather bottle and shielded his eyes from the glare of the African sun. He appeared confused for a second, as if he had heard something, then stared straight into the screen. He had seen the drone.

The man shouted angrily and a dozen other smugglers were by his side in a flash.

They were all toting guns. The men each had the same model and were already firing at the drone. It must have been remotely controlled because it flew above the torrent of bullets below it, gaining more altitude. Unfortunately, one of the men had managed to hit one of the drone's rotors. Black smoke trailed in front of the screen as the drone descended.

Tom caught a glimpse of the ground rushing closer towards him before the tape was cut off. Tom remained sitting on his chair in silence. This was all somehow linked to the people who had broken in. They had wanted the CD, along with the papers.

Tom removed the disc and held it in his hands as if it was made from gold. He found an empty CD case and kept it in there. Then he went back into the secret room and grabbed the papers.

As he was doing this, the telephone downstairs began to ring. The ringtone was simple and clear. Along with the papers, Tom stomped down the stairs. The telephone was on a wooded table with a socket above it. It was painted black and was vibrating heavily by the time Tom reached it. He picked it up and spoke, "Hello? This is the Cinnamon Grove."

The person on the other end of the line was female. "Hello! We are looking for Mary Flashfire. Is she in the house today?" the lady spoke gently to Tom, yet in a firm voice that made it clear she was in control.

Tom's mother! Why did they want her? "Sorry, she's not. She's at work. Who are you?"

The lady ignored his last question and replied, "You must be her son, Tom. We have a report on Jacob Flashfire who I take is your dad." Tom was perplexed.

"Yes..." he began. "I'm Tom. Is everything all right?" What could have gone wrong?
"I'm afraid I've got some bad news. I'm Ms Challaby from ISIO. Intelligence, Spy, Information and Operation. This is our postcode."

Ms Challaby spoke a long strand of numbers and letters into the phone. "Got it. Is it a meeting?"

Ms Challaby said, "Yes. We would like to speak to you so you can tell your mother everything when she gets home from work. It is your holiday's, right?"

"Mmm." Tom grunted. It hadn't been a very merry Christmas so far. He recalled the address. "I'll be there in... fifteen minutes."

"Great! See you!" Ms Challaby put down the phone. The second she hung up, Tom had raced up the stairs into his room. An ocean of thoughts were wild in his head. His father was in some sort of danger. It was bound to be something to do with the smugglers. "I should have known!" Tom mumbled as he ran into his room and threw open his cupboard. The lady had sounded quite important.

Tom put on a blue polo shirt and black jeans. He walked out of the room and put a brown leather jacket on top. Tom pushed on some trainers and remembered to grab the box- it had the bullet, knife and camera. The lady seemed to know what she was doing and could use the evidence for some investigation. He also grabbed his black school bag, emptied it and shoved in the papers and disc. He was ready.

Tom stepped outside into the hurricane. The trees were swaying side to side, specks of water landing on his jacket. Tom turned it inside out and continued walking outside the gate. It was arctic at this time of year, and Tom shoved his hands in his pockets. There was something in there. The second bullet! Tom comfortably curled his hand around it.

Tom had written down the address and realised it was nearly two miles away. It was too far to walk in the turbulent conditions. Tom turned back around and crunched over the gravel to his racing bike. It had twenty-three gears, a modified electric bell accessed by a button on the handlebar. The wheels had extra grip for the road. The chains were recently polished and the light frame repainted. Tom put the tin in his bag and proudly climbed on. He began cycling. It would take him half the time now.

There was no one on the streets, Tom noticed. Quiet. Eerie, almost. Tom shook his head and continued cycling. It wasn't far now. For some reason, Tom felt himself pedalling as fast as he could. Something was going on. His instincts told him that. And, on cue, Tom heard a faint whistle in the air and his tyre popped.

Tom sighed and climbed off the bike. There was a hole in the rubber of the tyre. It was probably a nail left on the road or a sharp twig. That was great. Tom upturned the bike trying to shake out the object which had pierced the tyre. It fell out onto the road.

It was another bullet.

Chapter 8

Tom backed away from it as if it was a poisonous snake. His aggressor had to be near. Tom was in a dilemma-freeze, fight or flight. Tom made his decision and turned to run. He smashed into the man standing in front of him. Tom hadn't seen him before but at first glance Tom could tell he was a smuggler. The man was even more intimidating than the one who had broken into the Cinnamon Grove. Tom gasped and fell back. He grabbed the tin and bag, stumbling. "Ok kid. I don't know who you are and don't care if you're just a child. Not interested."

The man wielded authority over the teenager cowering in front of him. "What do you want?" he tried not to show his fear. He wasn't going to let the criminal better him. The man laughed maliciously. "You're a kid. What could you do?" He drew something out of his jacket, leather like Tom's but black. Tom heard a click as it was reloaded. "Ok. We can do this the nice way or hard way. It's your choice, kid. Of course, if you were a man I wouldn't have given you the choice."

Tom could already tell that this wasn't going to end well. He knew what the man wanted. He remained quiet. "Ok, here's the deal. I want that tin. And the bag. Drop both of them. Now!" Suddenly the gun was pointing at Tom. "I'll give you three seconds. Here, look. There's a silencer on the gun. No one will hear anything, unluckily for you. Three!"

Tom's mind was racing with thoughts. He was out of options. He had to surrender. "Two!"

The man's finger tightened on the trigger. Toms stood up and held his hands above his head. He sighed. "You win, I guess." Tom dropped the bag and the tin. He saw the man smile wickedly. Tom kicked the tin towards him and heard it scrape across the pavement. "Good! Now we've come across to my way of thinking!" As he bent down for the box, Tom realised how bulky and muscular he was. Bulk. That was Tom's nickname for him.

Bulk's smile faded slowly. Livid, he turned to stare at Tom. "There's nothing in here!" he roared. Tom smiled at him. "Nope." He was holding the knife which he had concealed in his jacket pocket before he had left the house. The camera and bullet was in his bag along with the papers and disc.

Not wasting any time, Tom lunged forward with the knife. He spun it round in his hand and struck the man on the wrist. Bulk cried in agony, dropping the gun. Tom hadn't broken his wrist, but it was enough. He slipped the knife into his jacket pocket and grabbed the bag, sprinting away at full speed.

Adrenaline was pumping through his body as he ran. He heard the man screaming both in rage and pain. It was a small distraction and soon the man would regain control. He still had the gun. And his long legs allowed him to run faster than Tom.

But Tom had a clear advantage. He knew the ins and outs of the neighbourhood. Tom heard another whistle as a second bullet grazed him on the elbow. Bulk was a professional. Tom suddenly dived to the right into the hedges. The leaves and thorns tore at his face and the branches blocked his way.

But Tom fought through like a wild animal. Soon, he came to a small path in the middle of the hedge. He was covered in scratches and was bleeding but he would make it out alive. On his knees, Tom crawled through the uneven path, the branches shadowing him. He ignored the spasm of pain in his knee as he banged it on a root. His leather jacket was soiled and mud was in his eyes. Tom burst into the outside world in a flurry of leaves. The main road.

Tom laughed and collapsed onto the dripping grass. He was certain the man couldn't follow him through the hedge. It was too tight of a squeeze. Yet he had to keep moving. Bulk could have just ran around the hedge, which would only take a couple of minutes if he was fast enough. The main road was crammed with taxis and saloon cars. The dirty smell of the city hung in the air and thousands of people were irately dragging toddlers along the road as they watched the other shoppers, brightly wrapped presents spilling out of their tote bags. Now, this was more like London.

Tom clipped the bag to himself and slowly jogged to the roadside. It was too busy. The man would have caught up with him by the time he had crossed the street. He needed another way. The endless traffic didn't cease. He was trapped.

Tom ran along the grass. No one would stop for him. He knew the smuggler tailing him could easily make him disappear unnoticed by the crowds. The usual cars were horning the next and Tom couldn't hear himself think. Then he saw it. There was a black Mercedes-Benz GLS 63 AMG- one of the most expensive models of Mercedes in the world. Under the hood of the GLS 63 was a twin-turbocharged 4.0-liter V-8 engine that made a monstrous 603 horsepower with the help of a 48-volt hybrid system. All-wheel drive was standard, as was a nine-speed automatic transmission and air suspension.

Apart from that, it was just like seeing any millionaire on the road. The windows were tinted black and Tom couldn't see the person sitting behind them. It was slowly approaching them. Just then, while the luxury car got closer, Bulk reappeared. He was right behind Tom, holding a small pocket knife which he must have used to cut through the hedge. He appeared out of breath but was already running at Tom.

The Mercedes seemed to speed up. Bulk was coming closer. Tom was cornered by the man who had haunted him ever since his father had left. Tom wished he was there now. Someone was shouting at Tom from behind him, seconds before Bulk stabbed out with his knife.

Tom rolled to the side and lashed out at him with his foot. His heel slammed into his shin. Bulk roared in pain. Behind him, the window of the Mercedes slid open, revealing a kind-looking African woman. She was wearing thin gold-framed spectacles and was adorned with cheap jewellery. "Tom! Get in now!"

The back door of the Mercedes automatically slid open. Tom scrambled for the door as Bulk slashed out at him. It cut into the tough leather of his jacket, scraping against Tom's bare skin. Tom had no idea who the lady or how she knew his name. Bulk limped forwards- Tom had hurt his shin badly.

Headfirst, he dived into the Mercedes, landing on the cushioned seats which were already warmed from the heaters under the seats. But Bulk wasn't done yet. Tom twisted round and tried to shut the door. Bulk had grabbed hold of it and was tugging it open. He was stronger than Tom, and was winning the short battle.

The African lady was worriedly shouting to Tom but he couldn't hear her. He was too focused trying to stop Bulk. Tom let go of the door and the smuggler fell back. He was speedily back on his feet and hooked a hand around the door as Tom slammed it shut. "Aaargh! The man clutched his hand and fell back as the door smashed into his fingers.

Tom shut the door and put on his belt. He didn't have any time to enjoy the sixty-four colour ambient lighting, the plasma TV or Tri-zone climate control. He saw his saviour slam down on a button next to the driver. Tom realised it was the same man who piloted the Blackhawk. But instead of a jumpsuit, he was now wearing a thick winter coat and jogging bottoms.

Abruptly , everything outside went dark. It was a smoke bomb. Tom felt himself thrown back into the comfortable seat as the car accelerated. The squeal of tarmac on the road was accompanied by gunshot. The chauffeur stepped down on the pedal harder and the Mercedes raced away from the main road onto the pavement.

Tom was certain that any moment they were going to crash but the chauffeur was a surprisingly good, yet a dangerous driver. The lady sitting in front of Tom hadn't said a word yet. They were still in the middle of the action.

"Shoot!" the driver peered into the wing mirrors. "Miss, they're on our trail hot." Indeed, Tom saw an ominous-looking, black car that he didn't recognise parallel to them. It was a heavy Jeep which looked like it could turn the Mercedes into a piece of scrap metal. It was open-roofed and a bald man with a face wrap covering his mouth peeked up. He was holding a shotgun and Tom ducked as a spray of bullets clanged on the windows. Astoundingly, they stayed intact.

Finally the woman started talking. "Tom. Hello, I'm Ms Challaby from the ISIO. Fancy having you for the ride!" She was as calm and composed as if they were just driving to the beach. Tom didn't reply and was still staring at the windows, waiting for them to shatter under the impact from the onslaught of bullets. "Oh, don't worry!" she waved a hand dismissively. "I've done this plenty of times. The glass is bulletproof. Let them try."

Tom tried to speak but his mouth had gone dry. He nodded. Someone had tried to break into his home at three o'clock in the night, shot at him and now he was part of a ridiculous car chase which involved shotguns and smoke bombs. An unusual holiday so far!

The Mercedes swerved to the left as another Jeep, this one silver bashed into its side. Tom covered his head. Ms Challaby seemed composed and simply pressed down on another button. Tom heard a screech from behind him and saw the car had released oil all over the road. The Jeep slid across the tarmac before crunching into the plastic barriers on the side of the road.

But that wasn't all. Three men suited in black, head to toe, were tailing them on bikes along with the first Jeep. Tom didn't see a way out of this. Now he knew what it felt like to be in a movie. There was an explosion outside of the car- one of the motor bikers was armed with explosives.

Tom looked ahead. There was a pile of logs obstructing the road. He thought the chauffeur would opt for a diversion but was heading straight for the pile. Tom braced himself for the impact and squeezed his eyes shut. They collided with the stack and wood flew in all directions. A log rolled behind them.

The Jeep easily crunched through it but two of the men on motorbikes were unlucky. They were knocked down and Tom heard an explosion and screaming of metal behind him. Now there was one biker and the Jeep left. The biker was getting dangerously close.

They couldn't go any faster. The bike, however, was now neck with the Mercedes. Then the man riding it did the unexpected. He cautiously climbed onto the seat and was now standing on the motorbike still trailing forwards. Tom gasped. The stuntman jumped onto the car. Tom heard a thump above him.

"That's just great!" Ms Challaby shouted. "He's on the blasted roof! I have no idea how they do it!" The driver of the Mercedes, whose real name Tom didn't yet know, swerved around the road but the man on top of them wouldn't give. Tom saw a dark silhouette above him. The man was lying on his front, clinging to the roof.

Ms Challaby spoke calmly. "Tom, this is what you're going to have to do. I will open the roof in a few seconds and the man will fall in. See, there's a rope sitting next to you just there." Tom had earlier noticed it on the seat next to him. Suddenly he knew what was being asked of him. He nodded and held it up so Ms Challaby could see it in the rear view mirror.

"That's the one. I want you to tie him up with it then throw him out. It sounds stupid, but it's our only choice. You ready?" Without waiting for an answer she slid open the sunroof. Tom gulped. The man tumbled into the car, flipping around. His black boots slammed down on another red button next to Ms Challaby.

As Tom grabbed hold of the man, he saw a sleek object fly past him. "No! The headlight missiles!" Ms Challaby screamed. There was an explosion in front of the car as large pieces of tarmac erupted from the road. The man's bike was knocked of the road, smashed into pieces, hidden in the undergrowth.

The debris was followed by a wall of flame. In this time, Tom had somehow managed to restrain the struggling man, but not before he had managed to strike Tom on the chin with a strong punch. Tom's teeth were in pain and he tasted blood in his mouth. He wrestled with the man as they headed to the inferno. The Jeep was still continuously nudging them off track and Tom wondered what the expensive car model would look like after the ride.

For Tom's benefit, Ms Challaby opened up the door using a switch on her door handle. The air rushed into the car and for a second Tom was blinded. The man was tied up around the hands and couldn't move. Using all his strength, Tom shoved him out. Now his head and torso were outside, but his legs were still trapped.

The Jeep had taken advantage from the situation and was firing into the open door. Tom felt bullets whizzing past him as they embedded themselves in the leather seats, fluff flying everywhere.

Ms Challaby watched with apprehension, before being flung back into her seat violently. The man driving had to swerve to avoid a burning branch ahead of them. While doing so, the smuggler in the car was thrown out onto the road with a muffled shout.

Tom hastily shut the door before the men in the Jeep decided to take another shot at him. The warmth returned to the car and Tom breathed in, relieved. "Good job Tom-" Ms Challaby shouted over the roar of bullets and screaming tyres.

A burning piece of debris, from the aftermath of the blast, had set everything on fire. A heavy log smashed down onto the window screen and glass shattered over the Ms Challaby and the Chauffeur. He was thrown back into his seat and remained unmoving. The log was on fire, and the car had started to catch. Ms Challaby couldn't move without contacting the flames.

The driver lay there, unmoving. Tom kicked the driver's seat but he still wouldn't wake up. "Is he-" Tom began apprehensively. "No, thank goodness." Ms Challaby replied. "He's only unconscious." It was like she had no idea what scale of trouble they were in.

The Jeep had stopped behind them, but no one exited it. "We have to go!" Ms Challaby said urgently. "Maybe I can reach the wheel..." she leant over and reached for the wheel as someone in the Jeep took aim. Ms Challaby cried out and retreated her hand. She had been shot through her broken window, which had shattered on impact with the tree. The fire was creeping inside the vehicle.

Tom saw that they had shot her on the hand. It wasn't too bad, but she wouldn't be able to drive. They had got them.

Tom peered out of the window. There was Bulk, holding a Mauser C96 semi-automatic pistol in his hand, grinning vilely. Tom gritted his teeth. What had he got himself into?

There was only one thing left to do. Ms Challaby had produced a cloth and was wiping away the blood from the welling wound. "Are you okay?" Tom asked. "Oh, I'm fine. It just hurts a little-" She winced but managed a small smile to show she was alright. Yet, she sank back into her seat and from the sound of her breathing Tom could tell that she was unconscious, too.

"No, no!" Tom was flustered. He was alone with Bulk and the rest of the Smugglers. No matter how hard he tried, nor Ms Challaby of their faithful chauffeur awoke from their daze. Tom calmed himself down. Ok. Jacob Flashfire had taught him to drive. And he was trapped in a car with deadly smuggler everywhere. It was simple.

Tom removed his seat belt and climbed between the two seats at the front. He gingerly moved the driver to the side, allowing him some space to sit down. His dad had taken him for a couple of early driving lessons, so he got the general idea. A few buttons, a gear stick, a steering wheel, an accelerator and a brake. Easy.

Tom adjusted the seat slightly forward and was in the perfect position. By now, the men had started to climb out of the Jeep, each carry a machine gun. Without hesitating, Tom slammed down on the brakes and swung the steering wheel to the side. The Mercedes swerved to the left and a few smugglers jumped back, confused. Tom activated the windshield spray, and the fire was put out. He was ready. Tom ineptly jolted forward into the burned-out log. Wood smashed everywhere and Tom felt himself cut by splinters. He was driving very slowly, unconfidently. There was no shield between him and the guns. Bulk shouted and fired at the car. The bullet harmlessly pinged off the door but the metal wouldn't last long.

Now Tom began to pick up speed. He was getting the hang of it. He thanked his father for the car lessons that could save his life. But he was only a child. And the smuggler party had regrouped inside the Jeep, following him. Tom pressed down on the accelerator and the car sped forward. He let go and it jerked to a stop.

He was a sitting duck. The smugglers could tell an amateur was behind the controls. They could easily pick him off. The Jeep was just following him at that point. Tom saw the needle of the speedometer move up as he sped along the straight country road. London was far behind them. Tom raced ahead of the Jeep, getting more sure of himself. Apart from veering off the road a couple of times into trees, Tom was doing fine. Then came trouble. The road cut off to the right, creating a dangerous hairpin bend. It was going to be too close.

The Jeep bashed into the Mercedes, sparks and shrapnel flying everywhere. The two vehicles were driving over a bridge, with a raging river underneath them. Tom knew he wouldn't make it out alive if he didn't do something now. Instinctively, he slammed down on the black button, releasing the second lightweight missile from the headlights. It curved around, and for a second Tom thought it was going to hit him.

But it barely missed him, exploding in a tremendous firestorm behind him. Tom saw the Jeep flipped up into the air as the bridge gave away, tossing it into the torrent below. Tom watched as the car was washed away bit by bit. The smugglers had seen the missile and had evacuated the car, but a couple of them were struggling in the water trying to climb back onto the road. They had forgotten about Tom. He had made it!

Tom stepped down on the accelerator but he couldn't move. With dread, he realised the rear wheels were hanging off the edge of the bridge. The car, along with him, were going to be decimated. Tom had come so far but then this. No matter how hard he pushed, the car wouldn't mount the road.

He felt it slipping back. He only had a few seconds. Tom pushed one last time and finally the car was back on the road as the concrete from the bridge fell into the river. Tom was still accelerating, though. The hairpin bend was just ahead.

Tom tugged the steering wheel to the right.

It came off into his hands. "Are you serious?" Tom screamed. The log must have broken some part of it. The car continued skidding forward. Tom had no time to scream as the Mercedes-Benz GLS 63 AMG crashed into the trees ahead.

Chapter 9

"Tom! Tom are you ok?" The blinding light flashed down into Tom's eyes. He groaned and rolled around on his bed. He was in pain. Also, he started to remember the events prior to this. But he was safe in bed now. Maybe it was all just a bad nightmare. Tom groggily opened his eyes. He looked around him. He was in a hospital room, lying on a comfortable double bed.

Tom looked down at himself. The places where he had cut himself were bandaged. His chin had a plaster on it and there was a cast around his leg. Tom was aching everywhere but apart from that he seemed all right. Tom tried to move his right leg but winced in pain as he did so. Tom saw his now scratched watch lying on the table next to him. It was five, presumably in the morning. Everything was black behind the thin white curtains. Next to the watch there was a tray of food with some cheese and pickle sandwiches, a pudding and a glass of steaming milk. He was in a hospital.

Tom noticed the nurse standing next to his bed. She was very short, barely taller than Tom. Her hair was a rat's nest and there were bags under her eyes. Tom read the name badge pinned to her chest. Nurse Mary Addams. Nurse Addams caught Tom looking at the badge and spoke in a tired yet cheerful voice, "My parents named me after Mary Seacole. I always wanted to be a nurse." She smiled.

Tom tried to reply but found himself too tired to move. He sank into the bed. "It's okay. I've given you some medicines and you're recovering very quickly." Tom tried to nod. "My leg..." he croaked, pointing at the caster. "Oh, you've just sprained your ankle, dear. I'm sure it's a little sore but the good news is nothings broken."

Tom rejoiced. "How long..." He yawned. Tom was still in the state between sleeping and consciousness. "Only a few days!" the nurse gave Tom another flashing smile. "Now I'll leave you to rest for a bit. I'll wake you up in a few hours. Sleep well!"

Tom took a sip of milk and fell asleep once again.

***

"How is the boy?"

The question was directly fired at the woman sitting in front of a computer analysing a footage. Ms Challaby replied, "The poor dear is still in hospital. But he's recuperating unexpectedly fast, thank goodness!" The lady typed a message into the computer with her left hand. The other was hanging limply in a furl of bandages.

Jonathan Turner nodded. "Good. Though, frankly, I expected you and Mr. McLain to manoeuvre through those smugglers, not leave it up to a fourteen- year-old boy. And what about the Mercedes? We haven't got millions of pounds lying around to fix every blown up vehicle we have."

Ms Challaby sighed, ashamed. "We were both knocked out. There was nothing we could do. But that boy, he's amazing... Just like Jacob said. See this!" She held up a tattered rucksack. This had evidence on the smugglers and he found the papers and the drone footage. The smugglers couldn't find it, but a child of his age could."

Turner disregarded the backpack. "It doesn't matter. That was all for nothing. What if the smugglers followed you back to HQ? And the boy? He could have had far worse injuries because of you!" He shakily calmed himself down and said, "We just need Jacob back. Desert Ghost will fail."

He picked up the remote lying on the glass table, next to his cappuccino. The sixty-five inch plasma TV fluttered into life. The Mercedes was racing along the road, followed by the Jeep and motorbike, all displayed in HD. The man had jumped onto the car, and thirty seconds later he was rolling across the road into the bushes. Jonathan Turner skipped a few minutes into the action. The car was now much more clumsily driven across the road. The missile exploded into the road and the Jeep was thrown into the river. Turner skipped past the rest of it until the Mercedes crashed.

He had no emotion on his face as he watched. "The boy has potential. With a bit of practice-" He pointed at the screen. "We could have a new recruit on our hands. Jonathan's deputy was horrified. "We've already put him in enough danger. Tom also has his holiday! I've watched too many movies where a teenage boy is sent out on secret missions and no good comes of it!"

"We'll see. The squadrons are leaving at seven sharp in two days, understood?"

Ms Challaby nodded sullenly. "Fine. But if he says no, its no. And don't fire George McLain. He's been working here for years. It was just a mistake."

"We can't have mistakes at ISIO, Ms Challaby. You get that fact right. The sooner the better."

***

Tom was escorted down the carpet stairs of St. George's Hospital. It had been a few days since he had awoken in his ward, and was now all ready to go. He glanced at his watch. It was half past ten. Tom unsteadily walked into the austere waiting lounge. It was empty, apart from an old man on a walking stick hobbling outside and a nurse darting in and out of the wards, announcing a name on the loudspeaker. "So tardy." Tom heard her grumble.

As Tom left the compound, he thought about the events that brought him where he was now. And despite his efforts, he still didn't find out what had happened to his dad. Tom stepped out into the sun. While there were no clouds and the sun was shining, London was in the grasp of a bitter cold.

Mary came to stand by him. "You'll be alright getting home? You don't want anyone to pick you up? After all, you're hurt."

Tom shook his head. "No thanks. I'll be fine."

Mary smiled. "Okay. Your bike's over there." ISIO had found Tom's mountain bike on the path. Tom was surprised it hadn't been stolen. He said his goodbyes to the nurse before mounting his bike and racing off back to the Cinnamon Grove.

The phone call came just after Tom had finished his microwave lunch. It was the second phone call Tom had got after returning from the hospital. Ms Challaby had presumably informed his mother about the accident. Sophie Flashfire had begged the head doctors to take the day off to make sure her only son was alright. She was a very useful doctor and they wanted her to stay.

Though Sophie's bosses had refused, she had spent all of her lunch break on the phone talking to Tom. He had assured her that it was nothing major and he just needed to rest for a couple of days. Sophie had said that hopefully she could spare a day or two in the holidays to come home. There was still nearly two weeks until Christmas.

After finishing the bowl of Macaroni cheese, Tom had received the second call. It was a man who called himself Hawk. He had revealed nothing else about himself. Tom was told that the evidence had been salvaged from the wreckage of the Mercedes and everyone at ISIO was pinpointing where the smuggling operation could have been taking place.

Hawk had also mentioned that a car would be picking him up a few streets away from his home. They would take no more chances. Tom was demanded to speak to Ms Challaby. The tension was too much. He just wanted to get it done and over with. Unfortunately, Tom's leather jacket had been ruined in the crash so he had nothing smart to wear.

He threw on a shirt and a pair of jeans before leaving the house. But this time, he was more careful. He had learned his lesson. Bulk had been following him since he left the house. He had guessed that Tom had been carrying evidence.

Tom silently made his way to the gate. Nothing. The name of the street Hawk had given him was only a minute's walk. ISIO had deliberately chosen to not park right outside his house, in case there were any smuggler lurking around. As Tom left the house, he noticed people around him. There was a man wearing a long black tail coat, with sunglasses and a bowler hat. His face was completely hidden.

Without Tom noticing, he grabbed the boy and pulled him into a dingy corner in between some houses. The path was blocked off by a solid brick wall. Tom shouted and kicked, swinging his elbow round at the man's face. He ducked, then dropped Tom. Instantly, Tom flicked out a jab at the man. His incognito captor blocked his punch, grabbing hold of Tom's fist and lashing out at his leg. Tom was overpowered by the man and was on the floor within seconds.

He laughed. The man hadn't hurt Tom but he was still dazed. "You're good! I guess Turner was right about a new recruit!" He held out his hand. Tom, stunned, took a while to comprehend what had just happened. He recognized the voice, though it was slightly different on the telephone. It was Hawk.

Grinning, Tom took his hand and stood up. "Wow!" he began. "You scared me!" Even though Tom had been infinitely careful, Hawk had still bettered him. What if that was a smuggler? Hawk laughed again. "Yeah. Sorry about that."

Tom inspected the man for the first time. He appeared different to how Tom had imagined him. He was clean-shaven, muscular and had a short brown hair which spiked up in the wind. He reminded Tom of an international boxer, no older than twenty five. He had taken off his coat to reveal a blue and white striped shirt, stretching across his biceps. "Why did you stop me?" Tom questioned, a little angrily. While Hawk was on his side, Tom wasn't amused by the trick he had played on him.

"There was some suspicious activity going on around this area. Looks like the smugglers still haven't left you alone. It was much safer this way." Tom nodded. He was getting closer to finding out what happened to Jacob Flashfire. "How will we get past the smugglers? I had trouble escaping a single man."

Suddenly, it was in Hawk's hand. He had produced it out of nowhere, showing how deadly the ISIO agents could be if they were confronted. "Hopefully we won't need to use this." he glanced at the pistol. "Your father had another way."

He was facing the brick wall. "I know this will look simple, and I bet you've seen this a thousand times in movies, but..." He stretched his hand out and pressed on the unmoving snail that seemed glued to the wall. "The snail's a fake. Watch." Tom was amazed.

It was similar to the flip door in Jacob Flashfire's office. The wall of moss-encrusted bricks began to move slowly, grinding together to reveal a pass through the wall. At closer examination, Tom realised that the walls were not built from brick but merely painted to appear so. His dad had invented this? Using something like a snail as a secret button. It was ridiculous, but the perfect getaway. As the hidden door grinding open, Hawk went on. "Of course, the snail has a small camera inside its shell. It won't let me in before giving me a complete eye scan. You never know who might be watching us..."

The door had completed its transformation. "After you, sir." Hawk joked. Tom stepped through the doorway. He had always wondered what was behind the wall. Now he knew. There was a flight of stairs leading underground, made of cracked concrete. Hawk grinned and pulled out a torch. "In you go." He beckoned with his torch.

Tom took the first couple of steps down the stairs. It was dark and smelled musty. The circle of light from Hawk's torch wasn't much comfort. Tom's footsteps echoed in the gloom as he wandered further into the tunnel with Hawk following him. Each sound was amplified by ten and soon the outside world was a distant dream.

Tom heard the drip of water from the roof of the tunnel. With every step, they were travelling further underground. Tom even started to wonder if this was some sort of trap; that Hawk wasn't who he said to be.

It was all the same for what seemed like an eternity of walking before Tom's trainers crunched on glass on the path. Tom's eyes had adjusted to the dark and he made out a huge dark shape ahead of him. Hawk came to stand next to him. "This is an abandoned subway. That's a train there."

He pointed into the gloom. To Tom, such a powerful machine seemed eerie sitting there, alone and uncared for. The glass from the windows had shattered and the body was battered, paint chipping off. Tom warily passed it. Lying a few metres behind the train, there was a carriage lying on its side along the track.

The torch beam illuminated the wreckage. It was a cargo train- coal littered the tracks. They continued past another ghost of the locomotives that transported goods around London. The abandoned subway was a graveyard for trains.

Chapter 10

Abruptly, Hawk stopped in his track. At first, Tom thought the man had seen something, maybe a rat. "Do you hear that?" Hawk asked. He cocked his head to one side. Tom strained his ears, trying to pick up any sound around them. There it was. A distinct, mournful cry. While it sounded far away, Tom knew whatever was making the sound was in the subway.

Hawk pulled out his gun. "Careful. Stay right behind me." He took a diversion into another tunnel with Tom following right behind him. Torch in one hand, gun in the other, Hawk turned around the bend...

The torch light shone down on the rag of brown fur lying on the floor. It was a fox. Tom breathed a sigh of relief. "Huh." Hawk put the gun away. "Just a fox." Hawk unstrapped the bag on his back. Inside, there was a sandwich. "My lunch." Hawk said to Tom. He ripped the sandwich in half and threw it down at the fox. "That little fellow must have wondered in. He'll be fine. The exit isn't far. Come on!" Tom took one last look at the fox wolfing down the meat in the sandwich before heading back on the main route.

After five minutes of walking, Tom saw the end in sight. A ladder leading to the surface. He started to run towards it but Hawk restrained him. "Don't celebrate too soon. The ladder could be rigged with a trap." He approached it carefully, looking around at the walls and floor for any sign of trip wires or traps. He gave Tom a thumbs up.

"All good here. Let's go." Gratefully, Tom ran towards the ladder and began to climb it. The top was blocked off by a trapdoor but Tom pushed it open, spilling into the blinding daylight. Tom smiled. He hadn't enjoyed the subway one bit. Blinking in the bright light from the street lamps, Tom stepped aside to let Hawk exit.

They were in the main part of London. The Londoners were already in the festive mood, with a colossal pine tree in the middle of the mass of shops and houses. Golden Christmas lights adorned the shops windows and Tom saw a sign saying SANTA'S GROTTO THIS WAY!

He wished he could have been there to enjoy the season. But Hawk had apparently not noticed the delights around him and was already buffeting Tom along the street. Tom wrapped his jacket around him. "Another ten minutes, and we'll be there." Tom and Hawk walked through the streets together and soon the wild festivities were left behind as they entered a secluded, quiet corner of the square.

There were still shops and houses, but all the attention was drawn towards the main square. "Why are we here?" Tom asked. "It's in that shop." He pointed towards a tedious-looking pottery shop. "Our destination." They crossed the street and stood to face the pottery shop. It was purposefully made to not stand out, the grey words POTTERY SHOP stickered to the grimy window. The heavy wooden door had a sign hanging from the metal doorknob: SORRY WE'RE CLOSED.

Hawk tried to remember any single customer who had entered the shop in the last decade. Luckily for ISIO, nearly nobody had. Without knocking, Hawk pushed through the door into the shop. The lights were shut off and the cold wooden floor was lined with shelves, like in a supermarket. On the shelves were a variety of clay-sculpted decorations. Each of them were unpainted and of shabby quality yet with preposterous prices. Tom picked up a cracked clay cheeseboard which totalled to £339.99. No wonder it was an unpopular shop. But why had Hawk bought him here?

Suddenly, a woman appeared from behind the counter. "Great, you've made it!" It was Ms Challaby. She was wearing an apron on top of a Christmas jumper and had owl earrings. "Here's the boy as ordered, Madam." He smiled.

"Good work Hawk. You really should get a pay rise." She turned her attention to Tom. "Tom, dear, how are you? You know, you saved both mine and George McLain's lives. We really owe you one!"

Tom smiled. "Thanks. It was nothing." He turned around but Hawk was gone. Ms Challaby walked out from behind the counter. "This is the perfect disguise for the ISIO headquarters, Tom. What do you think?"

"Why a pottery shop?" Tom asked. To him, anyone could walk in and wander straight into the HQ. It was in the middle of London so there were bound to be tourists. "The main square holds all the attraction and we're always closed. No one ever dreams of coming here, though a rich foreign man once did a long time ago. He bought a little clay model of Big Ben." She held her fingers a couple of inches apart. "Sixty pounds. No one in their right mind would buy our products!" she joked.

"So ISIO, this organization you work for, operates here?" Tom asked.

"Yes, mainly. We have other quarters around the country but this is our chief office." Ms Challaby replied. Tom looked around at the sad pottery around him. He couldn't imagine that secret agents with sunglasses and guns were ordered across the globe from where he was standing. "Where's the rest of it?" Tom blurted out.

Ms Challaby smiled. "I thought you'd ask that. Follow me!" She stepped behind the counter and pulled out the cash box that was hidden under the table. She pressed down on the numbers zero, nine and six. Tom knew what to expect. Similar to the brick wall, the floorboards were hinged. They began to tilt into the ground, creating a slope into the secrets below.

Tom stared. The pottery shop disguised so much, while also sitting in the middle of London during the festive season. It had remained unfound for all its existence. "Customers never come behind the counter. Why make your headquarters on a desert island in the middle of the ocean when you've got this?"

She put the cash box back and began to walk down the ramp. Tom hurried down after her. One more step to finding the answer to the question he'd been asking himself ever since Jacob Flashfire had left. By now Tom had pieced together that his dad had been harbouring evidence of the smugglers. If he was a business man, why would he do that?

Tom heard a muffled thump from behind him. The ramp had closed up. They were in. All of a sudden, Tom felt like he had stepped out of the Victorian era into the future. The walls were made of steel and panels of light were running across the ceiling. The floor was made of a shiny metal, and there wasn't a speck of dust. Every few metres, there was a thick metal door barring the way, which was unlocked by the swipe of a key card.

"Did no one manage to find this place?" Tom asked in awe.

"Nope." Ms Challaby replied. "It's top secret." They continued along the corridor before reaching a set of double doors. Along the way, there were other doors leading into offices where rows of men and woman sat behind a computer.

Once again, Ms Challaby passed through the door with a swipe of her card. The two entered a furnished lounge, complete with sofas, an air hockey table, a soft drink machine and a desk with a stern woman sitting behind it. And the potted plants which seemed to be in every office.

Tom had barely taken a step when the two men had grabbed hold of him, guns loaded. They were both Chinese, with prim suits and one with sunglasses, which was a tradition among all secret agents. "Who are you?" They enquired.

Unfazed, Ms Challaby held up her card. The men took a step back. "Proceed, Madam."

Tom saw one of the men wink at him as he passed. "They're just guards," Ms Challaby explained. "It's a routine procedure. This is a top-security ISIO base. We can't take any chances, so says Jonathan Turner."

Tom saw a faint hint of dislike in the lady's expression. Jonathan Turner was Ms Challaby's boss. She was second to him in the hierarchy of the intelligence service. She strode towards another door and pushed it open. Ahead, there was another corridor with windows, showing of the posh offices inside of them. A lady burst out through a door. She had short red hair, an unusually long nose and was wearing a pristine lab coat.

She didn't notice Tom and urgently started speaking to Ms Challaby. "Our team has examined the drone footage and we have pinpointed the destination in the south of Algeria. Also, one more thing. We have spotted various parties of smuggler moving into the Sahara, and their trajectories are all leading to the same place. One of them must have-"

She glanced at Tom, as if afraid to go on. "They must have You-Know-Who! The squadrons have been deployed miles off track." Ms Challaby frowned.

"Send the signal to return to HQ. Tell them they're expected here by tomorrow morning. I'll be with you soon."

The lady left. "That, Tom, was Maria Selena. She's one of our scientists and it looks like the team has found a lead on You-Know-Who. Jacob Flashfire. Which is who we will be discussing." Tom gulped as they approached the last door in the corridor, before it led to a pair of double doors blocking access to a flight of stairs leading deeper into the complex.

The door was made out of metal, with a wooden coating. There was a brass plaque labelled DEPUTY HEAD. Ms Challaby pushed open the door. Tom was surprised. The Deputy of ISIO's office was unlocked. Tom remembered what secrets he had unearthed in his father's office. He couldn't imagine what was lying around in the suite which he was about to enter.

Ms Challaby stepped into the office and Tom was about to follow her when, "STOP!" Don't enter!" Tom froze. His right foot was half an inch from the office floor, which was steel-tiled. Tom withdrew his foot. "What?"

Ms Challaby was already in the room and nothing had happened to her. "The tiles on the floor are weight-sensitive pressure plates. If you step on one of them, the alarm will sound and the guns mounted into the suite's walls will activate." Tom took a hesitant step back. "Whoah."

"When we entered the shop, our faces and weight were recorded by some cleverly-placed cameras and weighing scales. For example, underneath the welcome mat. The stats were sent straight to our security computers where everyone who leaves or enters the building is recorded. After all of what you've just been through, it wouldn't have been a pleasant end. Sorry I forgot to mention it."

Tom started breathing again. That was too close. Ms Challaby walked over to the table which looked just like any other in a conference room. It appeared similar to the table in Tom's house. The deputy head pulled out one of the drawers under the table, revealing a control pad crammed with identical buttons. She pressed on a series of buttons, and the security was lifted.

"You can enter now!" Ms Challaby called. Nervously, Tom walked into the room. "I'm going to turn the security back on. You're desensitised to it. Take a seat." Tom sat down at the table. The room had barely any furniture apart from the table and a few drawers, yet with maximum security.

Ms Challaby snapped her fingers. Out of the blue, a smartly-suited waiter wearing a black suit entered the room carrying a tray with orange juice for Tom and red wine for Ms Challaby. "Thanks, Bartlet." She dismissed him and the butler closed the door behind him. "The system's already ineffective against him. But don't worry, I trust Bartlet completely. Basically, in the HQ, there is no way for a security breach." She sipped on her wine.

Tom hadn't touched his juice. "So about...?" Ms Challaby put down the glass.

"Ah. Yes. So, I presume your dad kept you from his actual jobs with some cover-up. What was it? A Lawyer? Bank Investor?"

"No. None of those. A manager of a company that makes plane turbines." Ms Challaby's face fell slightly. She shook her head. "I thought he could think of a better job. Oh well, onto the point. You may have figured it out but your dad is an ISIO secret agent. This starts on the day where Jacob boarded the Blackhawk." Tom felt it strange for someone to mention his dad's first name. He was referred to as 'sir' over the phone and Jake by his friends and wife.

"We attach a tracker to every agent who we send out onto the field. We did the same with Jacob. His mission was to put a stop to some smugglers travelling across the desert. You might have heard about them in the papers." Tom nodded. "He was sent to find them, and when he did we would have sent in a squadron to parachute down onto his position and arrest them. Also, the man who was chasing you is wanted by many countries. He hasn't got a particular name to himself because he keeps changing his identity. The world would be a better place without him."

Tom asked, "And what about Dad?" Ms Challaby's face darkened.

"A couple of days after we sent him in, his tracker stopped transmitting to us. It must have been destroyed. We don't know for sure, but the smugglers could have kidnapped him." Tom stared at Ms Challaby. The news had hit hard. He had known something was wrong, but being tangled up with notorious smugglers in the middle of the desert was going too far.

"He had evidence and was a threat to the smugglers. They broke into your house to find the evidence. Now there's only one thing we don't know; what exactly they are transporting. It's something big and that's the second part of the assignment. One man couldn't stop them but maybe twenty can." she finished.

Thoughts were swirling around Tom's head. Something big being moved across the desert. Twenty men. A missing agent. Would the squads being sent out that sunrise be enough?

"Okay," he started. "You go and do that, but what about me?" It was obvious that Tom couldn't go back home since the smugglers knew where he lived and had already attacked twice. Now he knew that there was more than one enemy, it was doubtful that he could fend them off on his own.

"Yes. We have already made arrangements for you to be collected up by your mother who will take you to the hospital she works at where you can stay for a few nights until we give you the all clear. She should be here soon. It's nearly sunset. I was also thinking you might like to come with us." Ms Challaby answered.

Tom's mother! Suddenly, Tom felt his heart racing. He had so much to tell her and couldn't wait. He leapt off the chair and ran outside. And getting to go on a mission? Tom smiled at the thought of going to the real desert with a bunch of secret agents.   "Tom! Wait!" the Deputy Head shouted after him. But Tom had burst through the doors which apparently didn't need a card to clarify someone's identity if they were leaving.

He ran through the corridors until he reached the lobby, where the two guards were waiting. They stepped in front of him, blocking the way. Tom heard footsteps behind him belonging to Ms Challaby, who was panting as she stopped in the lobby, hands on her knees. "The boys these days, so fast!" she stopped in front of him. "Okay, dear. Off you go!"

The guards parted and let him through as Tom ran up the stairs and the ramp automatically lifted open, sending a cloud of dust billowing into the air. Outside the handicraft shop, there was a car parked. It was an ordinary Skoda Octavia Estate. Tom's mother didn't have time to go around browsing in showrooms so instead bought a practical, cheap car which didn't require much searching or maintenance.

The lights were still on, and a thin winter-clad figure emerged from it, wearing a thick coat and gloves above her immaculate work outfit. Before Tom had a chance to step outside the building, his mother rushed up to her and said, "Oh, Tom! Are you okay? I got the call from ISIO; they told me everything that had happened. Someone broke in? I can't believe it! Are you okay, love?" she asked again, kissing   him   repeatedly   on   the   cheek. Finally, she broke away and told him to sit in the car for a few minutes. Tom climbed into the vehicle and was about to shut the door when he heard raised voices. Or it was mainly his mother's raised voice in the argument taking place before him.

"No! Jake's gone and now you dare to send my precious Tom to the middle of the desert infested with smugglers! You people are just as dangerous as them!" And with that the red-headed surgeon turned and sat down into the car, slamming the door. Tom could see Mrs. Challaby, not angry, but looking at him with a somewhat mischievous grin.

Before they got to say goodbye, the car was already speeding off down the icy road.

Chapter 11

Tom angrily sat in the hospital bed sulking. It was a different hospital to the one where Tom had been sent after his 'road mishap' as his mother called it. She was, once again, on an intense night-shift but had given Tom a whole ward to spend the next couple of nights in. A whole plain boring ward with an outdated Television, no video games and a picture of Big Ben which he had already gotten sick of.

His mother had strictly prohibited venturing out to the middle of desert, no matter what the cause. There was no question after the quarrel that had just taken place. Long story short, his mother had decided to stop him having the adventure of his lifetime and thought it would be a good idea to lock him into a ward with nothing to do. Not even- Tom was surprised his thoughts were wandering that far- a book to read. That was Tom's situation.

Yet if ISIO could disguise a shop in the middle of London and have only sold one thing in ten years, they could help him out of here. That look on Ms Challaby's face gave it all away: be ready because you're in for a surprise!

Was one of the agents going to come in dressed as a nurse and sneak him out with the excuse of showing him where the toilets were? A trapdoor? But Tom couldn't think of any action movies which involved fourteen-years old boy trying to escape a hospital by jumping into the secret passage through a toilet, hop onto a plane and fly into the world's largest sand desert.

Tom sat up. he had been left a bowl of spaghetti along with a tub of raspberry ice cream and a glass of hot milk. Tom downed the meal, drank the milk and felt no point in staying awake any much longer so stepped into the bathroom in the far left corner of the ward where there was already some toothpaste and a toothbrush, still in its packaging, left for him on the window sill above the sink. After Tom had brushed his teeth, without changing into pyjamas he threw off his shoes and flopped onto the bed.

He was stuck. And there was nothing he could do about it. After the glass of milk, Tom was feeling drowsy and soon fell into a slumber, only sleeping his way into what should have been another boring day at a hospital playing table football in the visitor's lounge. It really wasn't.

***

The wind hammered on the rickety window pane outside Tom's ward. It was a monster trying to break into the room and get him. There was frost on the window sills, which had collected quickly in the night chill. The boy was laying on his front on the bed, the blanket pushed onto the floor.

The curtains were whipped up and down by the wind that was travelling into the ward through a slit under the slider windows, nearly touching Tom. Outside, the torrential rain blurred the view. Then, out of the blue, a small, spherical object fell into the room. It was too dark to tell where it had come from. It made a sound not unlike glass shattering as it hit the floor. Tom, though, was in too much of a deep sleep to notice.

There was a pause. Then another came dropping down, shattering. The sharp sound was breaking into Tom's dreams. Smash! He turned uncomfortably in his bed. Then one more came falling down, and by the time it had smashed Tom was awake, pushing aside the blanket and groggily turning on the lights. "Wha-what?"

Tom slipped into his trainers and peered over the end of the bed where there was a collection of glass shards all over the floor. Tom looked up to see where they had fallen from. Why would someone through glass into his room? One piece was still moderately intact- Tom saw that it was a glass marble.

Above the mess on the floor, there was a vent. It was fairly large and Tom thought he could fit himself in easily enough. The vent would have to lead to somewhere! Someone was rolling those marbles down the vents from somewhere else in the building. And Tom had a pretty good idea who that someone was.

The question was how he would get up there. The walls were completely smooth, reminding Tom of a cliff he had once seen with a waterfall running from the top- the water had completely smoothened the rock over thousands of years. Ms Challaby had left the hard bit up to him.

Tom returned back to his bed. It was on wheels, but still very heavy. He was able to push the bed a few inches towards the wall with the vent. His plan was to jump up to the vent and pull himself in. Tom climbed onto the bed and took a final look to make sure he hadn't left anything behind. Then he took a few small bounces, before jumping up and hooking his fingers onto the edge of the grilles.

Unluckily, the vent was very loose and with Tom's full body weight depending on it, it came tumbling down with Tom. Tom flailed his legs and arms, trying to get another grip but he was falling. He landed on the bed, unharmed. The vent cover clattered onto the floor next to him.

Tom froze. Someone must have heard. Luckily, the holler of torrential rain sound-masked the bang. Tom fingers were sore from holding onto the vent, and he couldn't try to get another good grip without hurting himself. After massaging his fingers for a few minutes, he was ready to go again. He had the height- Tom just needed the strength to pull himself up.

Tom leapt. This time, he managed to get a secure grip and using the wall, he shuffled his feet up towards the vent. Then he stuck his head in, followed by his torso. But he was slipping. Painfully, he slid himself further up the vent so he could get his whole body inside. He had to be slow and careful, otherwise he would fall. At last, Tom managed to get his whole body inside the vent.

He stopped to catch his breath, and the side of Tom's stomach was aching from the strenuous exercise. When he had caught his breath, Tom pulled his Smartphone out of his pocket and turned on the flashlight. The dark vents were illuminated, and Tom could slowly crawl forwards.

Ms Challaby hadn't made it easy. All the time he was attempting his escape, Tom couldn't help thinking of his mother who would come into his ward the next morning to find no one. Further down the vent, Tom heard squeaking. A rat. The hospital definitely wasn't the most hygienic.

His elbows and knees banging on the steel, Tom crawled forward until he reached a point where the vents split, leading into other rooms and corridors. He had no idea where to go. He pointed his phone around looking for clues in the grimy, claustrophobic tunnels. The floor was coating in a thick brown dust, now also matted to Tom's clothes. In the patches of dust, Tom noticed streaks which had left a cleaner path behind them. That was where the marbles had rolled from.

Tom followed the streaks through the rest of the hospital, hoping no one would hear him as he bruised his elbows and knees against the walls closing in on him. The marbles couldn't have been thrown in from too far, otherwise they could have fallen through the wrong vent, or rolled down the incorrect path. Tom felt cold creep up on him like a ghost hiding in the vents. He knew he was close.

Tom shifted around a corner, and a few meters away there was another vent built into the wall. That was his destination. Motivated, Tom crawled forward quickly and reached the vent. He could only imagine the amount of dust coating him. Tom, with a little bit of effort, prised the vent off. He eagerly poked his head through the gap... and flung himself back with terror. There was no room. It was a fall. A long fall. Tentatively, he crept forward and peered down at the blackness. He was several stories up and that was no jump he could make without getting seriously injured.

Below him, Tom heard movement. Who was awake at this time of night? Tom guessed it was one of the nurses. He had to be silent. He was above a ward with doctors below him and no way out. If anyone caught him, he was going to be sent back to his ward and then there was no question of escaping. Where was Ms Challaby? Where was Hawk?

"Hey!"

Tom heard the voice calling softly to him. "Tom!" it whispered. Daring another look down, Tom found himself looking at Ms Challaby, who was hissing to him from her window. It was her! "Great, you made it! I tried not to make it too inconspicuous, so you would know it's me and not some prankster. Why don't you come down?" With some difficulty, Tom turned himself around in the narrow vents, lowering his feet until they rested on the window ledge. He was terrified, though Ms Challaby could have been acting as if they were two neighbours chatting together on a Sunday morning.

Gripping on to the sides of the vent with his fingers sticky with sweat, Tom slowly lowered his legs down, cautiously balancing them on the window sill. Ms Challaby took a few steps back, allowing him space to enter the room through the open windows. Tom's legs were now fully inside, nearly touching the floor. He wondered what someone would think if they saw him. A monkey who had escaped from the zoo, probably.

Tom instinctively let go of the sides of the vent and slid into the room, scraping his back against the searing radiator, which was turned up to the maximum level. He landed nimbly on the carpet into a small room, which, unlike his ward, only had one bed. It was a private suite. Tom realised he had been holding his breath ever since he had climbed down from the vent. He let it go in a swirl of icy air.

"Great job, Tom! I was worried the marbles wouldn't get to you but I had everything worked out." Ms Challaby said. Tom nodded his thanks for being freed. "Yeah. So, where are we?" Though his mom had worked here for years, Tom was completely unfamiliar with the layout of the hospital. "This is a suite I booked for myself specially. I managed to wangle a room underneath your ward. I had it all worked out. Look, I even cooked up a lie about twisting my ankle." Ms Challaby shook the cast on her leg that Tom hadn't previously noticed. "Mind you, the doctors didn't think anything was wrong with me. I insisted it hurt a lot, so they put a cast on and said I could stay the night even though there was no sign of bruising or external damage."

"That's great. One question: in the space of nearly half an hour, I've managed to make it down one floor of a 18-storey building. What's next on the agenda?" Tom replied.

Ms Challaby casually started unwrapping one of the mint chocolates the staff had left her. "You know," she began. "I was studying some diagrams of the hospital's sewage system..." Tom looked down at the floor, his face going slightly green. "I was kidding! Well, they definitely won't be too happy to see me around here. I have a feeling your mother had a word with security. As the deputy of ISIO, it's not moral to steal children from their beds in the middle of the night. Don't worry; It's easy from here. I just brought you down here to give you a little private briefing."

"So, we exit the hospital an there'll be transport waiting for us outside. The squadrons are on a tight schedule so we'll have to hurry. This is gonna be your first big mission- let's see if we have a new recruit on our hands!" she finished. "Let's bust out!"

Tom followed her out of the lavish ward, into the dingy corridor where one of the tube lights overhead was broken. They walked down the threadbare carpet past many cramped rooms, luckily meeting no nurses along the way who would question why two people were walking around the hospital in the middle of the night without supervision.

Ahead, there was a nurse carrying a trolley full of syringes. Ms Challaby confidently pushed open a door to the left and started walking down the stairs. Tom wondered if she'd been here before. The woman seemed to know the hospital well or maybe she had just studied some maps. They exited the stairway into the main lobby. The receptionist wasn't at the desk. Tom saw her inside a smaller room ruffling through some files.

"Let's go!" Ms Challaby said.

The lobby's lights were lit and Tom knew they would be caught if anyone entered the lobby. People weren't allowed to come and go at will; both visitors and patients had to declare their departure at the front desk. Tom hastily pushed the bright green button which opened the door. They both snuck out just as the receptionist walked back into the lobby.

Chapter 12

Tom groaned as his head hit the roof of the car again. It had been several hours since they had exited the hospital. Tom and Ms Challaby walked a few streets away from the building where there were a group of cars waiting for them. They were to be transported across England into the country where ISIO owned a runway, along with a hangar of aerial vehicles which they would use to fly to Africa.

There was nothing ahead of them on the inky black road. Nobody. It was nearing dawn and Tom felt lethargically tired. He had only gotten a couple of hours of sleep. The man driving their Jeep had a pair of ear pods in his ear and was bobbing his head up and down as he drove. In the front seat, Ms Challaby was sleeping like a log, also tired, while next to Tom there was a mean-looking bulky man who was about six feet. He was staring ahead his face permanently frowning as they approached their destination.

The gravel crunched under the group of cars as they rolled through countryside puddles and pushed pas the thorn bushes. Looking up, Tom could see a vast sky dotted with millions of twinkling stars. Stars winked at him from the endless arch of void-black beyond the moon's corona. In places they were birthstone-blue and beautiful, all glittering in their heavenly finery. The ones furthest away, almost outside the span of human comprehension, were like flashing pinpricks in a veil of darkness. They had a faint, silver tint and they looked like they were the distant, glittering sparks from a fire. It seemed to Tom that there was a snowfall sparkling in outer space and he felt privileged to witness it.. The browning grass serenely wavered in the breeze as the sleet-covered flowers stood in bunches like iced decorations on a birthday cake. Tom had never known such beauty could exist. London had never conveyed to him how amazing everything could be, even if his father was lost in the desert. But Tom knew Jacob Flashfire was strong. Nothing could stop him.

Tom carefully held the moment in his gaze before it was shattered by the sound of a car door slamming. Hawk emerged from one of the cars, along with all the other units dispatched for the mission. Now everyone had left the cars, Tom could see at least twenty people standing around him, all of them young men in camouflage or pilots with tinted goggles. Last of all, Ms Challaby, who was still slightly groggy from her sleep, stepped out of the silver Jeep.

All of the agents grouped together in their respective squadrons, standing by for order. "Listen up, guys!" Ms Challaby shouted to the group. "This is it. Our biggest operation yet. Two operations, actually. Get Jacob. That's priority. For his sake." Ms Challaby waved an arm at Tom. "Second, we've got to find out what the smugglers are transporting. We don't know what it could be; it might be pebbles. It could be money. It could be weapons. Mr Turner has requested we execute this operation with the utmost precision. But you guys can do it. Now, C unit you'll be taking the Bell AH-1Z Viper..."

Tom muted out Ms Challaby as she gave her orders to the different units. He was nervous. Very nervous. He had not done anything like this before. If Ms Challaby hadn't been there when Bulk was chasing him, Tom would have been toast. And she wouldn't be there in the desert. But then again, Tom had saved all their lives by outmanoeuvring the smugglers. Either way, this was going to be the most challenging thing he had ever done in his life.

One man. A 3.5 million miles squared desert. A hostile army of smugglers. Destiny had already lay out the path. Tom looked up in time to see a warm, golden sunrise spread its warming fingers across the landscape, the light pushing the darkness out of its way as the sky erupted with bursts of fiery colour as the sun rose higher into the scorching sun, the stars dwindling in brightness as the sun engulfed the beautiful morning sky. The distant horizon became a deep neon-blue as the sun began its steady journey upwards. The snow which had kept the dainty flowers captive for so long slowly melted with a scream fraught with agony.

The glorious sunrise had absorbed everyone at the scene. They were transfixed in its perfection until the crisp colours dominating the skies faded into a light blue. Finally, Ms Challaby broke out of the trance and regained control. "It's dawn. We have a few hours to get to Africa, according to the schedule. We'll make it in good time, if we leave now. Let's get going."

The units marched to their assigned vehicles as the aeronauts took their position in the cockpits. Ms Challaby hung behind with Tom until the units had boarded. "Tom, I won't be with you in the flight. I'm staying behind in England. But don't worry; you're in good hands. I've attached you to the B-unit, which is headed by Hawk. They're an experienced bunch, so you'll be just fine. You'll be heading out on a Bell. They're speedy things, so before long you'll be in Africa. It'll all be fine." Tom nodded, not so sure.

"Oh, wait. I have something for you." Ms Challaby produced a large duffel bag and handed it to Tom. He struggled with the weight and put it down. "It's got all the provisions you'll need- Food and water, clothes, a med kit... you name it. It's got the lot." She smiled proudly. Tom smiled back and picked up the bag.

"Thanks a lot Ms Challaby. This will really help." he said as a member of the B-unit took his bag from him and loaded it into the helicopter.

"Good luck, Tom. We'll get your father back. Just be careful, alright?" Ms Challaby said. "And also, don't worry about your mum. We'll deal with that situation, okay?" Tom nodded and stepped into the helicopter where four other men were waiting for him. Tom made his way over to an unoccupied seat and wore the headphones resting on the arm of the chair. This would help him hear the pilot over the noise of the engine. Tom felt himself being slightly lifted into the air as the rotors started spinning. Hawk reached across and slid the helicopter's stiff door shut. It shut with a bang, sealing Tom off from any hopes of going back.

The helicopter started flying up into the sky, wavering slightly as the pilot gained control. This was it. "Taking off." Even with the headphones, Tom could barely hear the pilot speak. The engine was roaring as they rose into the air. Tom saw Ms Challaby waving at him, a tiny speck on the patchwork of grass below. "Bye!" he shouted, even though Tom knew she couldn't hear him. Tom settled back into his seat and stared out of the window. He could hear the four men mumbling behind him.

Looking outside, Tom could see that the sky was turning blue. Small specks of snow were falling, instantly turning into water when they hit the ground. Soon they would have left the United Kingdom and they would be flying over the English Channel. In the meantime, Tom unzipped his duffel bag and rummaged through it. He had a torch, some sandwiches and the med kit in the first pocket.

Interestingly, he had been given a small pocket knife to use.

Tom was still tired from not having got a complete sleep, so put the items back in his bag and lay is head against the glass. *Hang on, Dad. We're coming for you.*

Chapter 13

Tom awoke with the harsh sun in his face. He looked away, blinded by the intense light. Shielding his eyes, he looked out of the window and was met with a sight. Sand. He was looking at a sea of sand. The dunes layered each other, forming perfect ripples in the sand. The desert filled Tom's line of vision. All he could see was sand. He had seen deserts in movies but they didn't compare to the majesty of the Sahara.

Tom already felt like the merciless sun was burning him. His long-sleeved cotton outfit provided a shield against the sun, but Tom felt the urge to pour water all over himself. The heat was unbearable. And they hadn't even landed yet. Tom ran a hand through his hair. It was sticky with sweat. "You alright mate?" Tom heard a voice crackle in the intercom."Yeah. It's just so hot!" Tom complained. The men smiled understandingly.

"Don't sweat it. No pun intended. We'll be there in-" Hawk whispered something into the intercom. "ten minutes. You need to keep hydrated. Take this." He chucked Tom a bottle of water. "Thanks." Tom muttered. He gulped down half the bottle in seconds. The baking heat had turned the water musty and warm but it was still a relief from the scorching conditions. Hawk laughed as Tom sucked the bottle dry. "Here, I'll take your bag. Put a few stuff in this rucksack. It'll be much easier to carry when we're down there." Hawk threw a rucksack across the seats. Tom emptied out his duffel and started sorting his items.

Then came another crackle of static from the pilot. "B-unit, do you repeat? Activity spotted down below. Do you want to investigate?" Suddenly, Tom's heart was racing. His father could be down there. Silence. Then Tom thought he felt a shudder below him. He shifted uncomfortably in his seat. Hawk exchanged glances with the other three men. "You don't think-" He began.

Then the helicopter lunged violently to the side. Tom shouted out with alarm. He was thrown against the window, which came close to cracking. Tom whipped his head around and looked down. He could see tiny dots on the ground and flickers of orange flying towards them. They were being shot at.

Another barrage of bullets embedded themselves into the helicopter. The four men behind Tom were on their feet, grabbing their bags. Tom felt the whole frame of the helicopter shudder. He pressed his nose against the Bell's window and could see a thick, disgusting plume of black smoke rising into the air. The usually composed pilot shouted into the intercom, "They've nailed the engine! We're going down!" Hawk ran forward and grabbed Tom's shirt as the helicopter tilted forwards. The B-unit slid down the body of the helicopter, slamming into the door of the cockpit.

"Tom, there's parachutes under the seats. Go!" One of the other men from the unit pushed Tom towards his seat. Tom scrambled up the floor which was moving under his feet and leapt onto his seat. He grabbed a pack from underneath his seat. He also grabbed his rucksack which he hastily tied to his leg. "What about you guys?" Tom asked. There was no way he could make it down there without them."Sorry Tom. We need to make sure you're safe. Just get out of here!" Hawk shouted.

Suddenly, the helicopter started drifting sideways and Tom was thrown against the door. In the cockpit the pilot was trying to gain control, pushing buttons and flicking levers. Maybe he could get the chopper level again before they came in contact with the ground. Then he was abruptly thrown back into his seat, kicking a button as he did so. The button which automatically open the door.

Back in the seating compartment, Tom was scrambling for a grip when the doors slid open, sending an immensely powerful gust of wind inside the helicopter. Tom couldn't even scream as the hurricane sucked all the air out of his lungs. He was being pulled. Tom had no idea in what direction he was facing because he eyes had teared up in the wind. Apparently, the parachutes didn't come with goggles. Tom flung his arms around him, trying to gain balance but as the helicopter lunged to the side again, there was no hope. He was falling.

Tom wrapped his arms around the parachute. He hadn't even clipped it on. It would be over if he let go. In the confusion and horror of the fall, Tom tried his best to find the cord which would activate the chute. Although all he could think about was the wall of sand rushing up to meet him. If he pulled the ripcord too late, he wouldn't have enough time to steady his fall.

Tom could feel the wind buffeting him harder and harder as the knot tied to his leg became looser and looser. The rucksack-which had a few precious provisions- would fall into the ocean of sand and be lost forever amongst the dunes. Tom, still not being able to see, miraculously found the ripcord and pulled on it as hard as he could. Once, he had a skydiving lesson with his father while a trained instructor had guided him.

He remembered the immense thrill and fear, but it was nothing compared to what he was experiencing now. The second Tom pulled on the ripcord, the parachute erupted into a silky mass of colour and he decelerated. Tom was now stably descending down into the desert. Now he was safe, Tom took the time to admire the magnificent view. On the horizon, there was a jagged line of rock which Tom knew were the Atlas mountains, named after the ancient Greek titan, Atlas.

Tom dimly heard the whirring of the Bell's rotors above him and twisted his neck around to watch the damaged helicopter sink further to the ground. He spotted no other bright parachutes gliding through the air which meant that nor the pilot or the B-unit had escaped the smoking vehicle. Tom knew he had to follow the general direction in which the helicopter was heading. He breathed in deeply and tried to remember what the instructor had said to him. She had said, "Left toggle to turn left, right toggle to turn right and pull down on both toggles to flare the parachute for a softer landing."

Tom pulled sharply on the right toggle, acutely aware that the parachute could have ripped and then it would all be over for him. While the Bell had lost a significant amount of speed, it was still going too fast for Tom to reach it. Still, Tom turned in the air and glided behind the helicopter as it fell. Maybe he could catch the crash and meet up with Hawk afterwards. Then they could send out an emergency call for help. Suddenly, the bag tied to Tom's leg slid off his foot and was now falling hundreds of feet to the ground. "No!" Tom shouted to himself. He had gotten too comfortable after activating the parachute and had forgotten about the bag.

He had to make a decision now. Bag or helicopter. Tom probably wouldn't make it to the helicopter in time and if he tried to tail it any further, he would have to trek the remaining distance without any of the essential provisions in his rucksack. Tom knew. Without hesitation, he pulled down on both of the toggles and began the journey down.

Tom was falling slowly, ensuring a safe landing. Already he could fell the sun hammering down on him. 15 meters, 10 meters, 5 meters... and Tom landed. Sand spewed up all around him due to the imperfect landing but Tom reckoned the instructor would have given him a pass. Instantly, Tom began looking for his rucksack which he had seen hit the sand not too far from him.

Suddenly, he felt dizzy. And he was sweating. Already, Tom was overheating in the intense heat from the sun. Temperatures in the desert could soar to 55 degrees Celsius. A human's body temperature only had to rise by around 3.5 degrees before heatstroke set it. And that was definitely not good news. The baking rocks, sand almost too hot to touch...this was the Sahara desert.

Chapter 14

Tom stumbled in the blistering sand, its heat which Tom could feel through his sturdy boots make him want to find shade. Tom was squinted in the heat and sweat ran into his eyes, the salt stinging them. He had only spent around thirty seconds in the desert and was already going crazy. Then an idea popped into his head. The parachute. It was trailing behind him in a deflated jumble. Tom ripped it away from the bag which had contained it. His first thought was to roll it around himself but he was smarter than that.

As he stumbled through the solid wall of heat, Tom spotted his bag. It was covered with sand but everything he needed was inside. Before looking for the item he needed, Tom grabbed one of the water bottles and chugged down nearly a quarter. It was the best water he had ever tasted. He screwed the cap back on the bottle and continued rummaging through the rucksack of provisions until Tom found the pocket knife. It was perfect for the job.

Tom held up the parachute. He found it surprising that it was made of silk because the parachutes he had used before were made of nylon, the modern-day material of choice for parachutes. But it was the right material. Tom grabbed the knife tight and started slashing. The knife glinted as it swished through the air, back and forth. Within another minute, Tom had a pile of roughly cut fabric at his feet. Tom picked up one piece, which was around the size of a scarf and started wrapping it around himself. Tom had already come dressed in suitable clothes for the desert: light clothes that covered his arms and legs and allowed air to circulate.

But he had no hat and his hands, neck and face were exposed to the harsh sun. After Tom had finished wrapping up, he piled the remaining silk into the rucksack. It would come in use later on. While Tom was hotter than he'd ever been, he had reduced the chance of sunburn and allowed himself a little more comfort. Because of the way he had wrapped the silk, the only part of his face visible were his eyes. After another swig of water, Tom was ready to go.

He could still see the fading trail of smoke in the air, imprinted into the cloudless, blue sky which would have been welcome back in London. Yet here the clouds could save his life. It was so ironic. "Where are the clouds when you need them?" Tom spoke out aloud. Luckily, the Bell hadn't crashed too far away and Tom had all the provisions he needed.

Tom said a quick prayer to the heavens. He was heading into what was possibly an inescapable furnace. But there were a whole platoon of agents out there. For one moment, Tom thought about calling off the expedition and giving Hawk a call from his phone. He pulled out the newest model of one of the most popular Smartphone series in the world. It was top of the class. And it was dead. Tom sighed a dropped the phone into his bag.

There was no other option. Just keep going. Tom started walking . Aside from the surroundings and heat, it was just like a normal walk. The silk protected him from the sun and Tom realised he wasn't sweating as much. Still, the work was taxing. After another hour of walking, Tom desperately needed a break. The sun was beginning its descent downwards, the same sun which had looked so pleasing and peaceful that same morning was the same sun Tom hated now.

He was tired. Exhausted. The smoke hadn't seemed so far away- only a few miles. But the reality was more like fifteen. Tom knew that if he had been wearing his watch, he would have broken the 10,000 steps target many times. He sank to the floor and pulled out the half of the parachute which was still intact. He lay it down on the sand like a picnic blanket and unzipped the bag. Inside, there were a few cans of tinned turkey stew, along with the sandwiches.

Tom pulled out a chipped tin bowl and a spoon.

Unfortunately, without a fire the canned stew would have to be eaten cold. Stabbing a hole into the lid with the pocket knife, Tom watched as the unappealing meal slopped into his bowl. While cold stew wasn't everyone's preferred dinner, it was better than nothing. Tom had purposely not poured himself a large helping because even though he was starving, food was less important than water. Too much food and he would be dehydrated.

Just as Tom was packing up, he thought he heard something in the sand close by to him. Something was hissing at him.   Slithering through the sand. Then he realised. It was just like the plane. He didn't understand what was happening at first, and then the worst possible thing that could happen would happen. Tom instantiy sprang to the ground. It wasn't too late to rectify his mistake. Tom grabbed the silk blanket and whipped it around in the air around him stamping his feet as loud as he could on the ground.

Out of the corner of his eye, Tom saw something slink off into the dying sun. His heart was racing as he dropped the silk. It was a saw-scaled viper. One of the deadliest snakes to have inhabited the Sahara. One bite from that...

Tom was angry at himself. He had come so far and one tiny mistake of not keeping an eye out for danger had nearly cost him his life. Spooked by the encounter, Tom shouldered the rucksack into which he had stuffed the silk into and set off. This time, he was careful to stamp each step to warn off any snakes possibly intrigued by him. The moment Tom got back up, he wanted to sleep. He was boiling and had nearly finished the first water bottle.

In the desert, the rule of thumb was to travel by night. The day was too hot. But he had had no choice. The sun had turned the sky into a sea of fire as it set. Night would be coming soon, along with its many dangers. Another half hour, and the Sahara would be plunged into darkness. But Tom decided to press on. The smoke trail would disappear into the inky black sky at night and he had to get as far as possible. In the bag, there was a pocket compass with a string around it. Tom took a second to get his bearings: he was heading North-East.

He let the compass dangle around his neck as he followed the smoke. It was almost certain that no one would be there. The unit, along with the pilot, would have left. But the helicopter would have provisions, means of communication and could maybe still fly. Tom watched the sun sink into the ground before resuming his taxing trek. Apart from the snakes, a diminishing supply of water and the heat, there was one more danger. The smugglers. They were definitely close- they couldn't have travelled that far after shooting down the helicopter. And that was only one group.

On the plus side, there were also many agents out there who would have got the word that a unit had gone down. Ms Challaby would have been contacted and all the force would be rerouted to find him. But then again, they could have no idea that Tom had been shot down along with five other men. They could still be heading in the original direction. Tom knew that there was no guarantee that help was coming. So he had to rely on his survival skills, handily taught to him by his father. Of course. Tom now knew why his father had taken him on so many adventures and trained him so much. He had passed his down his skills in case Tom ever was in a situation like he was now.

With those thoughts whirling around his head like trees in a hurricane, Tom approached the first of the dunes. The first one was around 600 feet tall. A dune of this immense height was called a star dune, hence its shape. Tom started walking up it confidently. Back home, he could have ran up it in a minute, if not seconds. Abruptly, Tom felt himself sliding backwards as the dune buckled under his weight. He tried climbing back up but fell flat in his face. Tom sat up and spat the sand out of his mouth.

Trying again, Tom found it slightly easier as he navigated through the dune. It was nothing like walking up a hill in the park. He had to use his brain and identify the shallower angles of the dune. Sometimes, there were no shallow angles so he had to backtrack and find a better route. By the time he was halfway up the hill, the sun had set, leaving only a weak tint of rosy pink in the sky. The world above him was a deep blue and Tom could already feel the chill of the night.

As the desert grew darker, Tom found it more difficult to see. At one point, he slipped and slid down five meters before regaining his grip. After a painstaking 30 minutes, he had at long last made it to the top. Tom felt like he would faint with exhaustion. He hadn't realised how thirsty he was getting and took a swig from the water bottler which was getting significantly lighter with each sip. Tom sank to his knees at the top of the dune. He needed sleep. Not waiting out the day was a mistake, and Tom would have to get down from the dune to set up camp.

Tom could feel his eyelids getting heavier as he rested at the top of the dune before a distant sound broke into his half-asleep daze. Shouting. Had they found him? Desert

Ghost or ISIO? Tom was instantly on his feet, pulling out the pocket knife. But the sound was coming from Tom's left. In the distance, there was a flicker of orange along with angry shouts. The sky had come alight as fireflies blazed in the distance. Tom could see men the size of ants darting left and right. Quickly, he pulled out the binoculars he had packed.

Tom zoomed into the fight scene. From what he could tell, a unit had run into a group of smugglers. A big group. Tom could see tents set up around the area along with a Jeep full of crates. Men dodged behind tents, some falling to the ground as their enemy's bullet found its mark. Tom saw a small ovular object thrown at one of the tents. The grenade exploded in a dome of flame as men were thrown back by the blast. Even with the binoculars, Tom couldn't make out the faces of anyone, smugglers or agents alike because it was so dark. In the distance, Tom heard a roaring engine as another Jeep pushed its way through the dunes. ISIO agents had been deployed only with helicopters, so they could quickly find the smugglers and parachute down onto their position. They had no other vehicles, so the Jeep held smugglers.

Four men couldn't stand a chance against the two smuggler groups. Hopefully, the other units would spot the skirmish taking place below and help them out. Transfixed, Tom continued watching the action. More shouting and explosions. Tom had seen the Blackhawk near the camp, which the unit had used to bombard the camp before taking control of the area. They were succeeding but it wasn't long until the Jeep arrived.

Without warning, the Blackhawk violently exploded, showering burning metal everywhere. Everything was on fire. A thick plume of smoke, nearly invisible against the sky, rose into the air. An enemy smuggler must have attacked the helicopter. The orange flicker seemed to be dying out from the right half of the battlefield as the smuggler reinforcements let loose a torrent of explosives and bullets. But what they didn't know was the Blackhawk had caused a chain explosion. Fire trailed from the first Jeep. It had caught alight as a tent had collapsed on it.

Tom heard screams of horror as the Jeep containing the shipments burst out in a bright inferno. All the shipment that the smugglers had been carrying had gone up in smoke- along with the Blackhawk, meaning whatever unit was locked in combat had no means of escape. Tom turned his attention away. In the space of a few minutes he was in a bad position. The battle which Tom had just witnessed was the closest, yet dangerous, means of civilisation. Any smugglers definitely wouldn't be happy to see him. He would be putting himself and the unit in danger if he went there. Plus, by the time he got there, Tom knew there would be no one left to help him. Frankly, the agents didn't stand a chance.

With this in his mind, Tom cautiously made his way down the hill. He had come to a decision. His destination was the Atlas mountains. There he could find help and communication. It was in the opposite direction to where the smugglers had made camp, which was the main reason Tom had chose to reroute his path. However, the wreckage of the Bell was not far and Tom knew that if he pushed himself, he could make it by Tomorrow evening. His provisions were running low already and if he was lucky, he could salvage enough to give him the boost to reach the mountain range. It was a big risk, but it was Tom's only choice. Unless he wanted to seek safety with the agents he knew could not help him.

He needed to move on. Tom pulled a torch out of the side-pocket of the rucksack. It was another risk. He knew how easily a single torch beam could be spotted in the distance. Tom twisted the knob to lower the brightness of the torch. He carefully made his way down the dune, knowing that the sand could collapse at any moment. As Tom drew nearer to level ground, he relaxed a little, taking more careless steps. Then he felt his foot snag on something as he took another stride.

He twisted round and shone the torch beam on the object. It was a rock. Tom cried out with pain as his foot dislodged itself from the small boulder. He dropped the torch and fell. He tumbled down the rest of the dune, sand flying into his eyes. Tom thumped onto the ground as he came to a stop. Another mistake. He had twisted his ankle on the rock because he wasn't careful. Tom knew it was going to be a serious impairment in the long run. Tom sat up, clutching his ankle as it burned. Luckily, he had packed a medical kit in the rucksack, which would relieve him of some pain.

With difficulty, Tom crawled towards the rucksack, hands trembling. It was freezing. Too hot in the day, too cold at night. The first thing Tom did was drag out a sweater which he threw on, along with a scarf and hat. He knew that the desert was cold at night but he had never imagined anything like this. Next, Tom unzipped the pouch holding the medical kit, pouring the contents out onto the sand. He had lost the torch- it must have broke when it hit the ground, therefore not shining its beam into the sky telling Tom exactly where it was.

The medical kit had gauzes, plasters of different sizes, tweezers, safety pins, sterile gloves and bandages. The kit also had an ice pack which would have been perfect for Tom's injury but it had long since melted into a slushy water bottle. The negative of that was Tom's twisted ankle would take a lot longer to heal. On the plus side, though, he had more water if he cut open the pouch. Tom unfurled one of the bandages and wrapped it around his foot, securing it with a pin. It would hold. Gingerly, Tom tested his weight on his injured foot. He would be able to walk, at least. But not for too long, otherwise he knew it would worsen.

Tom had no other choice but to set out to make camp for the night. He needed shelter, food, and a fire. He had packed waterproof matchsticks in the front pocket of the bag but he had no sleeping bag, let alone a tent. The silk was still in his bag, which he would later use as a mattress. Trying to ignore the pain in his foot, Tom packed up his possessions and began walking again. Even with the extra layers, Tom felt the cold bite into him, passing through any layers he futilely put on to try and block it out. Hypothermia was a disaster lurking in the shadows, waiting to pounce on Tom. He knew he would find so sticks, however, so Tom kept searching.

Eventually, Tom came across a dead bush. Its skeletal branches hung eerily in the glow of the moonlight. Using his knife, Tom shredded the bush into different sized twigs and sticks. He added them to his repertoire of provisions in his rucksack and set off again. Every once in a while, Tom checked he was heading in the correct direction. A careless wrong turn could take him miles off course and he wouldn't even realise because everything looked the same; the windswept dunes were leaning in the same direction, the stars over-cluttered the skies with no difference in the stretching band of glitter which was the Milky Way and no life. Nothing for miles.

The only thing Tom could safely rely on to track his direction was the compass. In the faint moonlight, Tom could just make out the two needles as they swung back and forth before coming to rest. Tom silently scolded himself. He was veering over to the North-East side of the desert, just slightly. If Tom hadn't checked, he would have gone round in circles until he dropped from exhaustion. He made a mental note to check the life-saving device every ten minutes. But he couldn't go another ten minutes. Tom reluctantly craned his neck up to check how tall the next dune was. Each was taller than the last, or so it seemed to Tom as his body became more tired.

No. Tom decided to trek around it. It would take more time, with a higher risk of losing track of his direction but Tom knew it was hazardous to climb up the dune in his current state. Last time he had nearly broke his foot due to him being inattentive. He needed to rest. Tom knew it was foolish to go on. Gratefully, Tom swung his backpack onto the floor. Not too far away, there were a pile of boulders which would provide perfect shelter from the elements. Last leg, Tom thought to himself as he hiked the last 500 meters. The warm fire he was about to make, another meal of stew and a much-needed sleep... Tom was motivated to reach the end point. At least it was the end point for today. Tomorrow was a whole new challenge.

Tom sank to the ground, slumping onto one of the boulders that had been washed there thousands of years ago by a river. There was a wadi nearby... Tom jumped. The rock was warm! After the hours of bitter cold he had felt, warmth! It was bliss. Tom let himself rest against the natural radiator, soaking in the heat. In the day, the sun warmed up the rocks. At night, those rocks released their heat. Possibly serving as a radiator for any 14-year olds who happened to wander past. Tom stretched out his injured leg, letting it rest. But he couldn't stop for long. Tom had to assemble a suitable camp from the jumble of rocks and items in the rucksack he had been provided with.

With some effort, Tom stood up and surveyed his surroundings. The best option was to set the rocks up in a semi-circle formation with the fire lit in front of him. It would provide him with some shelter when he slept and the fire could keep him warm and heat his food. Tom got to work. He cracked his knuckles and prepared to roll the first boulder into place. But, as he rolled the weighty rock across the sand, a small creature scuttled out from under the rock. Tom immediately leapt back, pulling out the knife and shining his torch at the spot where it had been. After recognizing the small scorpion, Tom scrambled up a boulder hastily.

Chapter 15

Androctonus australis. A yellow fat-tailed scorpion. Nearly as deadly as the cobra... Tom heard Mr Porryfield's words trickle into his head. As long as he was on the rock, Tom would be safe. Tom was perched upon the rock, weighing out the different possibilities. He could always use the extra food but he would lose more energy than gained from hunting it down, no matter how much protein it had. Tom also reminded himself that it was a deadly killer and he had to focus on defence, not offence.

Tom had to wait it out. Soon, the scorpion lost interest in the interesting human sitting above him and scuttled away. Tom sighed, waiting another thirty seconds until he was absolutely sure that the creature was gone. Tom slid off the boulder and continued working, checking under each boulder to make sure he wasn't going to get any more surprises. After a few minutes of adjusting the rocks, Tom had a vague semi-circular shape and a pair of aching arms. It would do for the night.

Tom set the rucksack down on the ground, which was getting evidently less sandy and more rocky and flat. This meant there were no dunes ahead which was a bitter-sweet gift. Travelling at night would be much, much easier but at day, Tom would have no protection against the blistering sun, apart from a silk parachute. But he would cross that bridge when he came to it. Tom pulled out of the rucksack the half of the parachute he had left intact. It was more comfortable than laying on sand, while also preserving his some of his body heat. Next, Tom started to work on the fire. He had taken the sticks form the dead bush with him, which were dry and around the right size to start his fire and provide fuel for it later on.

Tom had the waterproof matches, thought there was no danger of them getting wet. In his time being a Scout, Tom had learned how to make a fire. First, he needed the kindling- small, dry pieces of wood and other materials- to start the fire. He arranged them together in a small clump of kindling which would catch very easily. Tom struck the first match against the box again and again, but it was so cold that Tom's hand was trembling. He could see his breath dancing in front of him. The match snapped as Tom applied to much pressure to it. He added its remains to the pile of kindling. On his second try, Tom was lucky and had successfully lit the match. Cautiously, Tom drew the flaming stick closer to the pile of kindling. He dropped the match in the middle of the jumble and waited for the satisfying crackle that told him there was fire.

Tom watched triumphantly as a small flame burst its way through the wood, trying to escape. It was still a weak flame, however, so Tom leant over and gently blew. The flame burned more intensely as it grew. Tom waited a minute until he was sure the fire was of a good size. Tom fed the young beast wood to help it grow. Smoke rose and sparks spitted like in a blacksmith's forge. The firewood slowly crumbled to ashes as it was engulfed by the destructive flame which was ever growing larger. Smoke towered proudly in the air as the fire raged on.

Tom took of his silk wrappings and openly embraced the warmth of the fire. Arrows after arrows had been shot at him but he had made it this far. The smugglers, the car chase, the crash, snakes, scorpions and twelve hours in this furnace. But he had survived so far. Tom gratefully held his hands out to the fire, allowing the flames to lick his hands. Tom's face glowed a dark orange as he rested. His aching legs were soothed by his only companion roaring away beside him. Tom felt his eyelids grow heavy once more as he lay down. He could have fallen asleep within seconds, only if he hadn't been so hungry. Tom knew thirst was the biggest danger in the desert but to him hunger was a competent rival.

Tom reluctantly sat up and pulled out his chipped bowl and spoon, along with the tin of stew. It had been hours since he had last eaten and a meal would guarantee him a long, sound sleep. A bonus was this time he could have heated food. Tom set up a splint with the left over firewood, allowing him to balance the pot which luckily came with a handle over the flame. He had no foil to wrap the bowl in but it would have to do. Tom waited as the food was heated, passing his time by staring at the stars. He spotted many constellations, including the Big Dipper, Draco the Dragon and Ursula Major.

In the peace of the night, Tom found something niggling at the back of his mind. The fire. Its flames were a beacon to any passersby, including smugglers. But it was more likely for one of ISIO's helicopter's to notice the flame as it hovered above the sky. It was a chance. The units had probably all landed at that point, but it was possible that a few air patrols were looking out for him.

The smugglers weren't a huge problem. He was covered by the dunes that layered the extensive Sahara and the smuggler would be asleep- that is, if they had no knowledge on how to travel the desert. Walk by night and rest at day. That was the motto. Tom felt his stomach growl which reminded him of the meal being heated on the splint. Carefully, Tom pinched the rim of the bowl and lifted it away from the splint. He collapsed the splint into the fire as he saw the flame dimming slightly. Tom smacked his lips as he pushed his spoon into the steaming bowl. He had left it over the fire a little bit too long and he stupidly burned his tongue.

Tom took a swig of the water. There was only a quarter left now. The only other water source he had was a small 500ml bottle which he had thrown into the mix of items he had packed. The water in the bottle refracted the fire as it sloshed about at the bottom of the bottle. Tom finished his supper and packed his gear away. He would still be cold at night without a blanket, so Tom shook out the back pocket of the rucksack where all his spare clothes were. They would have to do as a blanket. Tom didn't want to waste water putting out the fire before he slept so tentatively kicked the pile. It collapsed and the flaming pieces of wood were strewn everywhere. Tom stamped out the diminishing flames and scoured for pieces of wood that were still burnable. He found a few sticks that were largely unharmed by the fire and put them in his rucksack. They would help him the next night.

Now on the verge of falling asleep on the spot, Tom crawled into the cosy shelter he had built himself. In another few hours, the shelter would be a oven when the sun warmed up the rocks again. And he would be inside it. Tom set an alarm on his watch to make sure that when he woke up he wasn't roasting. Tom untied his boots and sank into the silk. Tom imagined himself in his luxurious bed at home. What was happening back in London? Was the house being guarded? Did Ms Challaby catch Bulk? These were Tom's final waking thoughts as he finally fell asleep.

***

Tom groaned as the harsh Sahara sun burned into his face. He felt groggy and was slick with sweat. Tom felt something vibrating on his left wrist. It was the watch. Tom rolled over on his silk mattress. He was on his luxurious bed in the Cinnamon Grove and was sleeping in that Sunday. "Aargh!" Tom sat up, hitting his head on one of the rocks. It was burning hot. Tom clutched his head in pain, scrambling out of the furnace he had slept in. He had set his watch too late, because according to it he was still in the United Kingdom. A foolish mistake. Tom could barely open his eyes because of the unbearable sunlight. He shielded them from the sun, slowly opening his eyelids as he adjusted to the bright light. He felt a sharp pain in his foot

Abir Gupta

as he was reminded of the previous night's catastrophe. Tom made sure to change the bandage before doing anything else.

Tom checked his watch again. It was 10 o'clock, meaning it would be 11 o'clock in the Sahara because there was a rough 1 hour difference in the United Kingdom and Sahara desert time. In another hour- noon- the sun would be at its absolute hottest. Tom had to move quickly; faster than the heatstroke just around the corner. Tom's eyes were glazed. Feeling light-headed, Tom steadied himself. Water. He needed water. Tom unscrewed the cap and drank heartily. Tom promised himself that if he got out of this alive, he would never complain about the rain again. Or cold showers. Tom studied the water bottle. There was the shallowest of puddles at the bottom of the water bottle, allowing a few droplets to moisten Tom's lips. The situation was getting desperate. In the desert, the average human body needed at least a litre of water an hour in the desert. And Tom had to make half of that last for the rest of his journey.

Tom could feel the sun beating down on him harder each minute. He needed a shelter, and fast. Tom decided to build a simple makeshift shelter by propping up the silk sheet on two stick which would block the sun. And when the sun moved, he would move the shelter. Tom got to work, setting up the shelter so it blocked the sun. He had cut to circular holes in the silk where the sticks from last night's fire could be slotted into and tied on with his shoelaces. After ten minutes of working under the sun, Tom had a passable shelter. Most of the sunlight still got through into the shelter, however. The shelter wouldn't be effective without extra protection. Tom grabbed all the shirts, jumpers and trousers from his bag and layered them over the silk. This gave him much more protection. Aside from a few small tools, a meagre supply of food and water and clothes Tom had nothing to help him. The rest of the food, water and gear including sunglasses, sun cream and a stock of 2-litre water bottles were in the duffel bag which had much more space for larger items like his sleeping bag.

Tom reckoned the stew would last until dinner that night. After that, Tom would have to live off the land, something he was not looking forward to. Annoyingly, his duffel bag had enough cans of tuna to last him a week. But without the rucksack he would have come to a stop miles ago. He was no survival expert but knew a few things about hostile environments from books and a few short excursions. Tom lay in his shelter which was hot (around 30 degrees Celsius) but not overly uncomfortable. At sunset, he would begin travelling again. His plan was to climb a tall dune to get a suitable vantage point to spot the helicopter. Tom knew it was close. The Bell would have supplies and could provide him shelter.

Tom stared into the shimmering sky. On the horizon, Tom spotted what could have been a helicopter. He felt his insides fluttering with excitement. Was it coming this way? Tom squinted at the black dot as it grew smaller. It could have been a helicopter. Or it was just an illusion. In the haze, Tom could make out the rough outline of the Atlas

Abir Gupta

Mountains. They looked very close, like he could run there in 10 minutes. Tom knew, however, that it was just a mirage. The air was so hot that it distorted things in the distance and Tom couldn't trust the naked eye. Tom was staring out over the unforgivable desert. Day 2 had begun. Tucked away behind a small dune, Tom noticed something. Tracks. Most of the tracks had been erased by the wind but Tom was pretty sure they were tyre tracks.

Recklessly, Tom ran out of his shelter, ignoring the sun which had beamed all its heat at him. Tom reminded himself to slow down but excitedly trotted to the tracks. Yep. They were definitely tyre tracks. Tom saw the arrow markings created in the sand. They were pointing South, meaning the vehicle had been travelling North. Tom rejoiced. Civilisation was close. Then his blood ran cold. "Why?" he cried out to no one in particular. Smugglers. Of course. They had come here. They had driven right by his camp. Tom scrambled up the dune and scanned for any vehicles. The desert was as barren as ever. Tom hurriedly returned to his makeshift shelter. Nowhere was safe.

For the rest of the day, Tom stayed hidden in his shelter resting, pocket knife close. The grand sun rose higher into the air, until it stood at the tip of the universe like a deity shining down on everything else. Without bothering to heat up some stew on the fire, Tom wolfed down a bowl. The smoke was too much of a giveaway. *Please*, Tom prayed, *help me out of this.*

Tom laid back in his few square meters of shade. There wasn't much, but it was his. He made sure to watch out for snakes and other dangers. Surely, there would be scorpions fighting for shade but they would be wise to stay away from the boy with a knife. Tom knew he had little to no water so he would have to be clever and ration his supply. Once, Tom had read about a Mexican tribe called the Tarahumara. They made their water last a lot longer by holding it in their mouths and letting the liquid slowly soak into their mouths. It was a difficult practice but in the end, it helped them survive in the long run. Tom decided to take a small sip and hold it for at least fifteen minutes. He set another alarm on his watch and began.

At first, the water sloshed at the back of his mouth and because he was so thirsty, the urge to gulp down the water was almost too strong. Tom persevered. It was a good distraction from the sweltering heat. Tom felt his mouth starting to ache when his watch started vibrating. Gratefully, Tom swallowed the water. He had made it last so much longer than if he had just swallowed it down normally. This time, Tom decided to try a half-hour hold. His watch counted down the numbers. 3,2,1... Start!

Tom practised repeatedly until he was able to hold the water for nearly one hour. The Tarahumara managed to do it easily for hours on end but one hour might just help Tom get out of the desert with some water. They falling sun caught his attention as the Sahara Desert was lit up in a fiery glow. Already, Tom began longing for the sun as the cold crept up on him like a jaguar in the dark. Tom stood up, testing his ankle. Since the morning, it had healed greatly. Tom was able to walk just fine, the pain only a silent companion lagging behind him. He had recovered very fast- it must have only been a minor injury.

Tom took one last look around the camp. He was leaving. His goal was to reach the Bell before dawn. If he started now, Tom would reach it. As a bonus, his shelter for the day would be sorted. The stars glimmered into life as Tom finished packing up the camp. He had thrown on all the layers he could and had a quick meal. He was ready. Taking a sip of water which he vowed he would hold for as long as he could, Tom began walking. He always made sure not to stray too close to the tyre tracks which other smugglers could be trailing. Tom stared up at the stars, allowing himself a minute to rest. He needed the breaks otherwise his body would exhaust and there was no way that was a good thing. Tom had started climbing the dune he had spotted earlier to get a better view.

By the time Tom got to the top, his thighs were screaming in pain. Tom allowed himself to down his water as he pulled out the binoculars. In the dark, Tom could barely make out the dark shape that wasn't too far away. He would make it before dawn, surely. Inspecting it more closely, Tom could see the broken frame of a helicopter. His heart was racing. This was it!. He thought he saw something moving in the helicopter but he put it down to low visibility in the dark. Remembering the lesson he had learned last night, Tom carefully, walked down the dune taking firm steps towards flat ground. Near the bottom,

Tom slid down the rest of the dune on his feet and jumped onto solid ground.

Tom noticed a certain spring in his step. The helicopter didn't mean victory but it would definitely help him achieve that- or so he hoped. Tom felt the cold wrapping itself around him and was spurred on by the thought of a warm shelter, a shelter better than the pile of rocks he had slept in last night. The moonlight illuminated his destination in a silvery glow, the crescent revealed as invisible clouds moved out of the way. As Tom pushed onwards, he noticed his shoulders growing heavy with pain. Carrying around a rucksack for so many hours had took its toll. Tom breathed warm air into his hands. It was the last leg.

For the next few hours, Tom put himself into auto mode. He put one foot in front of the other and walked. Once he was into the flow, it was easy. A five- minute rest every hour, holding water in his mouth for one and a half hours and walk. That was all there was to it. However, Tom felt his stomach rumble in protest louder by the minute. He needed food. There was no guaranteed food left in the helicopter so he needed to scavenge for his own. The stew was running out and Tom decided to keep it as a reserve if things got desperate. There was nothing in sight for Tom to eat so he had to contend with an empty stomach for most of the night. At home and school, whenever he felt hungry or thirsty, he could pay a visit to the kitchen or cafeteria where there was always juices and snacks.

Even with just having had a sip of water, Tom felt himself pining for refreshments. He was thinking of people at the beach, lounging in their armchairs sipping on Coke and lemonade. The smell of fried potato chips wafted across the air along with the tang of vinegar. Tom's mind switched to another scene where a family were gathered in front of the television on a harsh Winter evening, enveloped in blankets with mince pies in their hands. But dreaming of home comforts only made Tom thirstier, hungrier and more frustrated. For every hour that he walked, it felt like the helicopter grew closer by a metre. For every hour that he walked, it was twice as hard to keep walking after a short break. Yet for every hour that he walked, he was closer to safety.

After an eternity of aching legs, hunger and thirst, the helicopter came into clear view. Tom strode into the lightening sky. A very thin trail of smoke rose from the wreckage. The helicopter didn't even look a kilometre away. Careful not to get too excited, Tom took another much-needed rest before excitedly approaching the wreckage. Even with a softer landing in the sand, the helicopter's days were undeniably over.

The nose of the helicopter had taken most of the impact and the windscreen had been shattered, leaving glass everywhere. The main rotor had cracked and was lazily lying in the sand. The tail boom which supported the tail rotor had been ripped off from the main body of the helicopter and was lying a few metres away from the main wreckage. Metal was everywhere. The landing skids hadn't done their job very well and were buried in the sand, only a few inches showing. The nose was battered and that was where the smoke was rising from. The interior of the helicopter was mainly intact, apart from the cockpit area which was still burning weakly. The impact of the crash had snapped the seats inside the helicopter. Tom felt his palms getting sweaty as he clambered inside the downed vehicle. He didn't know what he would find inside.

Tom tentatively navigated through the cockpit area, avoiding crackling wires and the fire. Suddenly, Tom jumped and whipped around. Something was rustling. Something, or someone, was still here. Tom picked up a broken metal pole that must have been part of the framework. "Hello?" he called, trying to be brave when he felt anything but. There was definitely something there. Behind that seat...

"Tom? Is that you?" A voice called from behind the chair. Tom edged forwards. He recognized the voice. It was weak, but he could still tell who it was. Tom ripped away the already broken chair to reveal a man lying on a bed made of seat cushions. His leg was wrapped in a bandage and he looked deathly pale. It was Hawk.

Chapter 16

"Hawk? What happened? What are you doing here?" Tom shouted worriedly, throwing aside the bar as his fear dissipated. Tom flicked open the pocket knife and started slashing at a seat that was laying on Hawk's thigh, eventually freeing him. The man was in a bad condition and his injury looked a lot worse than any twisted ankle. Hawk tried to sit up but slouched down. "Hey, take it easy!" Tom sat, forcing his water bottle into his hands. Tom ,concerned, examined Hawk's leg. He caught Tom's gaze and said, "It was injured during the accident. I think it's broken but the others bandaged me up and they said I'll be fine. I'm not so sure though."

"It looks kind of bad. Where even are the other guys?" Tom questioned. How could they just leave an injured man to die like that? That wasn't what team members are supposed to do."

"Well," Hawk croaked weakly, "After you jumped out of the Bell, the pilot told us there was no way of regaining control. He didn't even bother to send out a Mayday and grabbed the emergency hammer, smashed the window and jumped out with the last parachute. Don't think he's gonna last long, though. He's just an aeronaut and knows pretty much nothing about the desert. Plus, he forgot to take any supplies with him."

"Huh," Tom scoffed. "Didn't even bother to send out a Mayday? Serves him right for being so selfish. Maybe one of the other units picked him up?" Hawk helped himself to another mouthful of water before replying. "I hope so otherwise that's one more missing man we have to worry about. I'm so glad that you made it here. I didn't think you could survive- after all, you only had that rucksack. Not much water in there, right?"

Tom nodded. "It's been hard. But it looks like you got the short end of the stick."Hawk nodded sombrely. "The rest of the unit said we have a military base near here. I wrote this note for you in case I wasn't... you know, when you got here." He brandished a slip of paper with some nearly illegible handwriting, not unlike a doctor's. At least according to the doctors Tom had met. "Whelp." Hawk tossed the note behind him."Anyways, we got wind of the direction the smuggler are travelling from various units who are tracking them as we speak. There've been a few fights, too. We received an emergency call from the A-unit but it was cut off before any of us could hear what they were saying. A couple units have retreated back there after they got an idea of the smugglers' positions. But there are still over half of the suspects still remaining to be found. The guys have gone there to get help. They left me most of the food and water so I was good for the last couple of days. It's still a pretty rubbish situation for us all. Should have stuck with becoming an engineer..."

"Mmm. Do you have any idea when they're coming back?" Tom asked. Hawk replied, "They left yesterday so it'll be another few days before they come back. But I don't think they left me with enough supplies to last until then. We'll work that bit out later. So what happened to you?" Tom narrated his story to Hawk, everything from the scorpions, gunfight, his ankle and the tyre tracks he had found. The gunfight was the source of a big conversation. "That must have been the A-unit." Hawks started. "A Blackhawk, right? Did you see any survivors?"

Tom shook his head. "No. There was a big explosion, and then reinforcements arrived. I don't know what happened to them after that. Whatever happened, I bet it's not good!"

Hawk stroked his chin, deep in thought. "Those smugglers are pretty clever. They've probably got them held hostage. If I were them, I would offer a choice- one or the other. Jacob's is the official head of the A-unit, but ISIO usually attach him to various other missions as well. He's the more important man. For example, once he went solo to the middle of the Atlantic to investigate some illegal ocean drilling. We are the equivalent of MI6- don't tell them, but we're better than them! The cases and missions it took them years to execute we did in a mere few months. This is just like any other mission. Do you play chess? We've put our king into danger. We're like pawns attacking to save him."

Tom said, "One thing I don't get is what exactly are they transporting that would be so valuable to kill for? I think it's something big like diamonds or money. They would become so rich if they pull this operation off!" Hawk laughed loudly. His broken leg seemed to be forgotten.

"You think diamonds and money is big? Nope. We're thinking things worse than that. The problem is, we don't know. At least us two don't know much, being stuck in a crashed helicopter. Don't know what progressions the others have made. I guess we'll just have to wait and see."

Tom looked around the ruins of the helicopter. "Help is coming... but not for another few days. So do you think one of us should go and fetch help a quicker way? Wait, do you still have your Smartphone?" Hawk shook his head. He grabbed his bag and unzipped it. "Haven't got much, see? Phones were prohibited because there was too high of a risk of being tracked. Kind of ironic since we're supposed to do the tracking. Sorry about that. This palaver wasn't even supposed to happen in the first place. Now, us lot have had our share of survival training. It would probably be better if we stay here. After all, I can't really go anywhere."

Tom disagreed. "We don't know how long they'll be and to me it looks like they have most of the resources. Here, I have an idea. One of us should go fetch help because, to be honest, I don't think the rest of the B-unit is coming back any time soon. Look, there isn't much for us to live off so we'll have a better chance of survival if we split the food and drink so one of us will have enough to survive here while the other will have enough to get them to the base, where we can fetch help."

"You know, that's not a bad idea. Anyways, ever since I first joined the B-unit I had that feeling that the rest of the squad would leave me hanging if they ever got the chance. I think it's pretty clear which one of us should go." He chuckled, trying to stand up. "What! Are you crazy?" Tom shouted. "A broken leg and you want to go out in the middle of the desert?" He looked exasperated as he forced the wounded man back down to the ground. Tom pointed at his chest and declared, "I'll go. I have the best chance of getting there quickly. It'll be easier than what I just had to go through because I can pick up a few extra supplies. What do you say?"

Hawk sighed. "You're a lot more useful than I thought you'd be. I haven't got a doubt you will be able to reach the base but it is a big risk. I don't really want to send you out into that battlefield. We haven't even got weapons. All they left me with is this little pistol and a handful of bullets." Hawk shifted to the left to reveal a small gun with a tin of bullets next to him. "It might do if one or two of them find me. But if a truckload of them discover we're here this thing isn't going to be much of an assistance."

"I've survived them once before and I can do it again." Tom said adamantly, crossing his arms, challenging Hawk. "Ms Challaby ordered this: First, and most important, find my dad. Second, find out what they're smuggling. I'm pretty sure that doesn't cover, 'save Hawk'. No one is going to come. We either waste all our time here or actually try to survive." Hawk looked defeated. Despite Tom's earlier protests, he managed, with a lot of groaning, to stand up, putting all his weight on his healthy leg- the right one. Tom could tell he was trying to not cry out with pain. Through gritted teeth, Hawk said, "Fine. You're a stubborn one, just like Jacob. Two can play at that game. Without me, you're not going anywhere. Either both of us stay or both of us go. The choice is yours, Tom."

Tom knew he had to take the opportunity. This compromise was as good as he was going to get. "Fine. But we're not leaving until sunset. Or until you've got a proper treatment." Tom picked up his rucksack that was resting on a layer of dust. He brushed it off and unzipped it. He fumbled inside it until he found what he was looking for. The med kit. "I'm guessing they didn't leave you any extra bandages. He untied the string holding together a furl of bandages. Tom let the bandage uncurl in front of him until there was just enough to tie around Hawk's leg. He rolled up his trouser leg, pointing his finger just below his knee. "That's the spot." He said simply.

Hawk had already removed his previous bandage so Tom got to work straight away, wrapping the fresh dressing around his leg. He made sure it wasn't so loose it would fall off or so tight it would cut of his blood circulation. "Is that okay?" Tom asked. Hawk grunted a yes. He tried standing up again. "Thanks. It's good. But I'll need something to walk with because I can barely do anything right now. It hurts like anything. I'll try and find a walking stick..."

Tom had sticks in his bag but they were too short to support the six foot man standing in front of Tom. "Maybe a piece of the wreckage?" Tom suggested. Hawk picked up a landing skid and examined it. "This is the best we've got. But it is too long and the edges are jagged. I'll cut myself if I use that. We have nothing else, but it's not morning yet so we still have some time to scavenge for things we can use in from the desert. As we were plummeting down, I think I saw a date palm. We'll get dates there and wood- that knife of yours looks like it could cut me a pretty neat stick. So what are you waiting for? Let's go!"

Hawk took a step forwards, crying out loud in pain as his weight shifted onto his injured leg. Tom was about to help him, but Hawk held out a hand. "I'll be fine." He slowly dragged his left leg behind him as he limped out of the wreckage. Tom threw him a sweater but there wouldn't me much need for it after another thirty minutes. Tom could already see the distant sky burning. Pink tendrils were sneaking their way towards the pair as the sun ascended. "We'll bake if I don't hurry!" Hawk picked up his pace, still trailing behind Tom as he sauntered towards the tree.

Tom could see the top of the palm tree jutting out from behind a dune. Its majestic spiky leaves were browning but Tom could see clusters of dates hanging from the top. Instead of walking up the dune, Tom insisted on taking a detour around it. It was large enough to cause problems for Hawk's leg if they attempted to climb it. Tom recalled how painstaking the climb was and Hawk could easily slip without a firm grip with both feet. It added on extra time to the short trip but it was worth saving a worse leg injury. The date tree was tucked away behind the dune and now Tom could see it. He had eaten dates before but took a distaste to them- they were nowhere near as good as turkey stew.

Tom could feel the air warming up and knew they only had minutes before the desert became unbearable again. Hawk crashed to the floor, relieved of the punishment of walking with a broken leg. He sat up with his back against Tom's rucksack. "This is it." Hawk said. "By the looks of it, actually, I don't think we can make any walking stick out of that old thing," The date palm was around 9 meters tall, with a diamond-patterned trunk where identical hunks of bark overlapped each other, resulting in an armoured monster which looked almost impossible to climb. "Don't worry, though." Hawk continued. "You don't have much firewood in your pack but this is just what we need. You can strip away pieces of the bark and we can start a fire." Tom looked at him, befuddled. "How will that help?" Despite what he said, Tom already had his knife in his hand and was hacking away at the tree. Hawk smiled. "I've picked up a thing or two since I've started at ISIO. We can use the fire to weaken the bonds of the metal pole, melting it. Essentially, I just want to split them apart. Then we leave it to cool and hey presto! A walking stick." Tom looked doubtful and stopped chopping wood. "I don't know if that will work. But if you say so, sure." After another minute of hewing, Tom had a sizeable pile of firewood to start a sizeable fire.

Hawk helped him scoop the flakes into his bag. After they had finished packing up the would-be fire, Tom gave Hawk a sideways glance. "I was thinking finishing off a the turkey for brunch. A dessert would be nice to go with it, wouldn't you say?" Hawk looked at Tom quizzically. Tom turned to the towering tree and looked up at the dates hanging at the top, almost teasing him. "Oh no. You can't-" Tom was already climbing.

"Come down, Tom! I don't want dessert!" Hawk shouted frantically at the daredevil. Tom decided to ignore him and focused on climbing. It was all too easy to cut his hands on the bark. But if he stuck to the basic motto of three points of contact when climbing, he would be fine. Tom used the plates of bark as ledges to push off from. He had to wrap his arms around the tree and bring his legs up, shimmying up higher with each push. Tom felt the bark digging into him but kept climbing. Tom could feel his grip getting weaker, his palms getting sweatier but he kept climbing. "Listen, Tom. You still have the chance to get down now!" Hawk called.

As Tom neared the top of the palm, he felt in his pocket for the knife so he could cut down the fruit. Tom looked down, where the small blue knife was sitting on the sand. "Great!" Tom shouted. Hawk followed his gaze, his eyes settling on the small tool. Hawk was close to laughing. "I did tell you to not climb it." Tom shook his head and reached out to the dangling food. He tried to rip the wrinkled, vividly green clumps of dates off the tree. Tom felt pieces of bark snap under his weight as they fell to the ground.

"I've...almost...got...it!" Tom said between gritted teeth. Just as Tom was about to dislodge the first bundle from the palm tree, he lost his footing. In a frenzied panic, Tom let go of the tree and was falling through the air. In one split second, Tom managed to cling onto a cluster of dates. He was now hanging precariously off a ten-meter tall tree. If he fell, that would make two broken legs they would have to deal with.

Hawk was immediately up on his feet. "Don't panic, Tom. There's a place you can put your left foot a couple of inches down..." Still, clutching onto the clump of dates, Tom followed Hawk's instruction, taking weight off the bundle of fruits that looked like it could have snapped at any moment. "This one is a little further down. Tom, you can use the fruit to lower yourself down further." Tom edged down the tree, now relying once again on the cluster of fruit to hold his body weight.

It seemed to happen very fast. The dates which Tom was holding onto were all of a sudden no longer part of the tree. The result of that was a boy hugging some fruit mid-air ten meters high. Tom had no time to scream and was already half way to the ground. Hawk grunted and hobble over to the tree. Tom was going to land on his back- possibly breaking it if it hadn't been for Hawk. Tom felt his breath knocked out of him as Hawk caught him. The impact was too much for Hawk's injury and he crumpled to the floor with Tom in his arms.

Tom crawled away from Hawk before standing up and giving him a hand. Hawk's leg just couldn't take the weight. "Sorry." Tom said. "I should have listened to you." Hawk waved a hand dismissingly even though his expression conveyed the immense pain he was in. "No worries. I like dates. Where are they?" Tom looked around before finding the green ball which was half-submerged in the sand. Tom picked up his knife and handed the fruit to Hawk. "Here it is. Can you hold it up for me?" Tom sliced the bunch of dates until they were all separate. "That would have been handy earlier." he commented.

Together, they put the dates in Tom's rucksack. "We'll be snacking on those for weeks!" Hawks joked as they made their way back to the camp. The sun had begun to show some muscle so the pair hurried back to the helicopter. Tom glanced at his watch. It was nearly 11 o'clock. Hawk settled back into an upright seat as Tom began making the fire. He didn't have to waste any matches because the fire which was previously raging in the cockpit (Tom was surprised the rest of Hawk's unit hadn't put it out) had practically died out apart from a few embers nestled in the charred seat where the pilot would have sat.

Tom managed to get one piece of wood alight with the help of some seat fluff he had cut up to use as kindling, carefully carrying it outside before blowing on it to strengthen the flame. He cared for the fire until almost all the wood was gone and it was a powerful creature. It crackled and hissed as Hawk came forward with one of the landing skids in his hand. "Yeah, I don't think this is going to work. But what have we got to lose?" Tom said. Hawk just smiled and left the pole in the fire, careful not to place it so the whole fire collapsed under its weight. "I just hope this thing's melting point isn't too high. Even if it is, that won't be a problem, I think. That is one hot fire. Good job."

And so they waited. The sun was nearly at its full strength so the two of them prepared by covering up damaged part of the helicopter which could allow light in with silk. Hawk found more parachutes in the pilot's compartment, much to his annoyance he hadn't been offered them when the helicopter plummeting to a fiery end, which were yet to be put under the seats for passengers. Soon, the sun had very little space to shine through into the interior of the helicopter. The silk wasn't protective enough so Tom once again layered it with his and Hawk's spare clothing. After five minutes of being hard at work, the two of them stood back to admire their handiwork. "This is an adequate shelter for the day, you think?" Tom nodded. He went back outside to check on the metal pole. "I've had to sleep in worse, to say the least." Tom joked. "Hey, I think your pole is melting!"

Hawk dashed over and slid the skid out of the fire. The middle of the pole had almost completely liquidised. "This is so ridiculous!" Tom laughed. "No way is it going to work!" Hawk, his hands wrapped in silk to protect them from the heat, held both ends of the pole, slowly bending it. The liquidized metal dribbled onto the pole, solidifying. Tom looked on as Hawk snapped the skid in half, seconds before the liquid hardened again. He blew on the hot end to let it cool before presenting it to Tom. "You were saying?"

Tom took the staff in his hands. "Cool! I had no idea that that was possible." Hawk chuckled. "You learn a new thing every day. I can also use this as defence if it comes to that. So now we just wait for sunset and then we'll go.

Hopefully, I won't slow you down to much now I have this." He waved his staff in the air. Hawk thrust it into the ground and practised walking circles around the helicopter. "This will do just fine." He reported after another lap. Tom could see beads of sweat trickling down the man's forehead. It was already a sauna outside.

Hawk leaned his stick against a seat and sat down, unscrewing a water bottle. For a few minutes, the two of them rested their wounds, Tom applying plasters to his bleeding palms. They started sampling the dates, washing them down with mouthfuls of water. After a few minutes, Hawk started talking. "Ok. We're healthy and rested now but we have to talk about our supplies. We have at least a two-day trek ahead of us under a blistering sun. We don't have much firewood but we can cut up some more seat fluff so that shouldn't be a huge problem. We have a lot of things that burn. We also have these cans of tuna and dates to eat, which should last. If not, I know a few tricks that can get us some more food."

Tom grimaced. "Trust me, I don't want to know what's going on in your head right now. I have never eaten an insect and never will eat an insect." Hawk smiled mischievously. "This new generation is all pizza and burgers. What have we learned from our ancestors? Anyways. Water is the main issue here. We have about two litres to share between us-" Hawk watched Tom guzzle down more water. The Tarahumara trick seemed to be a thing of the past."A little less than two litres. No wastage. Let's set a timer on your clock to ration the supply."

Tom was sat relaxing on the ripped, de-fluffed, chair deep in thought. He was fiddling with a date in his hand, not eating it even though he was hungry. "Hawk," he said. Hawk looked up from the chair he was cleaving. "You know the date tree? How is was it surviving?" Hawk put down the knife and started heaving the fluff into the amassing collection inside the rucksack. "What do you mean?" he asked Tom. "Well, the tree must have needed water to survive. Do you think there could have been water under the sand feeding the roots?"

Hawk shook his head. "Sorry, Tom. I had a look earlier. I dug down around a meter but the sand was as dry as a bone. But keep that in mind for the next time we find a tree or bush, alright?" Tom nodded his agreement. He slumped back into his seat, ignoring the uncomfortable angle the seat was sitting at. Beside him, Hawk was slicing away at another chair, making sure the night's fire would be sufficient for both of them. Tom was safe. Within seconds, he was asleep.

Chapter 17

Tom took one last look at the Bell. They would have to leave it in the desert to rot for eternity. "You served us well." Hawk said, rubbing a hand along the shattered windscreen. He straightened up and said, "Have we got everything?" Tom nodded. Food, water, clothes, tools and the sleeping bag. "It's all in there. All the seats have been de-fluffed and I transferred the stuff from the duffel into your rucksack. We're good."

"Cool." Hawk replied. "Remember, after this there won't be shelter. We need to make a temporary structure which we can pack up into my rucksack for tomorrow. Here, help me with this." Hawk lifted up the battered tail boom. We can use the two halves of the landing skids, along with this, to create a general structure for our camp. Then we drape silk or whatever on top." Tom and Hawk heaved the parts of the helicopter into Hawk's much larger rucksack. They jutted out from the top and the rucksack couldn't close, but Hawk said he could manage. "I think we can make a good distance tonight if we press on now. Shall we?" Tom nodded. Hawk rubbed his hands together. "Let's do this thing."

***

The black Jeep trundled along the desert in the moonlight. The five men sat bunched together on cracked leather seats, their weapons only an arm's reach away. They looked ghostly in the dark. All of them were wearing grimy camouflage, face wraps covering their mouths. A bulky figure hunched next to the driver had a scratched radio at his mouth. A distorted voice spoke, "A downed vehicle spotted at these coordinates..." The voice rambled off a list of numbers. The radio man nudged the driver, signalling him to change course.

A small man cramped into the corner of the Jeep cradled a crate. His peers were sternly watching over the newbie, the largest of them fiercely cracking his knuckles to intimidate him. The Jeep continued on its uneven path, rattling up yet another dune. Another, even fiercer man kicked at the driver's seat."Faster!" He growled. The driver growled angrily and stepped down on the accelerator and the vehicle sped off into the night. Within minutes, the Jeep neared the proximity of the vehicle that had been observed by another group of smugglers.

The driver slammed down on the brakes. Sand explode into the air as the men slammed their car doors shut. A small scorpion that had been seeking shelter in the helicopter scuttled off, alarmed. The first man kicked aside the tail rotor, clambering inside the bell. "We got them, alright." The small man announced gleefully. The driver turned around and confronted him. "Don't get too cocky, Ferdinand. Otherwise you'll learn the hard way what happens to those who are too overconfident. Now get in there and be useful." Ferdinand scurried into the wreckage, looking for signs of survivors. The large man who was looking over Ferdinand in the car held up his hand. "Get over here. I found something." The other four men crowded around him, trying to find what they had missed earlier.

Someone produced a torch, shining it on the grainy sand. "Footsteps. They survived. I told you to aim for the windows. We didn't want the helicopter down, we wanted the men down. "Hey, look." Ferdinand waved a hand excitedly at the sand. The four other men reluctantly trudged over to him to see if the fresh recruit had found anything of use. "Yeah. Footsteps. We've already found them, dummy." Ferdinand shook his head. "No. These footsteps are smaller. There was a child with them."

"Or someone could have small feet." The driver said, shoving him out of the way to investigate further into the ruins. The slashed seats... a missing tail boom and landing skid... The man angrily kicked at the helicopter. "They left ages ago! It must have been days since they've gone. Couldn't those guys get me the coordinates a second earlier?" The other four men ignored him and continued searching, knowing listening to their driver's tantrums would do them no good. They continued poking around the wreckage. "Look." one of the smugglers said. "We're trying to get out of the desert, not getting into trouble. We are being hunted so this piece of junk is no use to us." The smugglers were getting frustrated. They couldn't agree on their colleague's logic. "Yeah, but we need to know where they're going so we don't run into them, genius. There has to be a clue as to where exactly they've gone."

The driver emerged from the cockpit grinning wickedly. "Oh, there sure is!" He showed off a small slip of paper he was clutching. "Those fools left it here. It says: *Tom, I wrote this note for you in case I'm not here when you arrive. There's a base we own North from here. It should take a couple of days to reach. I hope you get there safely- Hawk.*"

The smugglers laughed cruelly. "A base, huh? Seems worth checking out." one of them suggested. Another angrily retorted, "The agents will be swarming that place like flies! We have the shipment and you just want to turn up with it?" The first man was about to reply but the driver fired a shot into the air. "Stop! We do whatever I say. I don't care about some base. We know where they're going. Where they are. Coincidentally, they are also going in roughly the same direction as us. I saw two sets of footprints. We have the Jeep. With one of their people, we'll have some leverage over them if we get into any trouble before we reach the chopper."

"And what about the other man we caught?" Somebody asked. The smugglers had no idea how to work in unison. "Do you think the man they have will save us if we're in trouble?" the driver snapped. "It's every smugglers for himself out here. We're doing this for ourselves. No one will come running to save us if we need help. The targets may also know a thing or two about where the rest of ISIO are positioned. This'll be a piece of cake. Now get back in the Jeep. We have some hunting to do."

***

"Great, another dune!" Tom exclaimed. "Will you be able to make it up?" Hawk nodded before stowing his walking aid into the rucksack. "That stick is no use on dunes. Come on." The moment Hawk started climbing the dune and applying weight on his injured leg, he collapsed onto the sand. Tom offered him a hand up. Hawk took it, spitting sand out of his mouth and dusting down his trousers. "That was not the best of ideas. We should go around." While this added time on their journey, Tom whole-heartedly agreed. Even he didn't want to face another dune. Again, there was a chance of injury and of course the fact their legs had to work twice as hard to get to the top. For every one step forwards, they took two backwards.

The sun had long since set and night had descended on the desert once again. Tom could almost feel the tension in the air. They were getting close to danger. Something big was coming up. Tom looked up at the stars, praying his dad was alright. It would take a miracle for all of them to get out of the desert alive. Tom was like an innocent fly who had walked into a spider's web without knowing it. What Tom didn't know was the spider was coming in closer for the catch. The smugglers were getting closer with every step they took. And they didn't need breaks every hour, being in a car.

Hawk and Tom didn't chat much. There was no point in wasting saliva- that was how desperate the pair were for water. Tom currently felt alright, thirstier than he would have left himself at home but not in a life-threatening situation where water was the only thing that could save him. Once more, Tom was in zombie mode where he switched his brain off and walked. Still, Tom had to watch for dangers. Hawk already knew about making loud sounds when walking to scare snakes but there were too many things to look out for. Was that a scorpion's nest they had just disturbed, or a rock that could have resulted in another broken leg?

Hawk convinced Tom that there was no need to be so incognito and gifted him with torchlight. Tom gratefully focused on the path ahead of him, without the need to scan for every little hazard under his nose. And so they walked. Tom felt no different to how he had felt the night before. Everything was well until Hawk stopped Tom. "Hey, look over there." Hawk extended his arm to point at the horizon. Tom followed the tip of his finger until he saw it. "It's a dust storm." Hawk told him. "I was in one once when we were out in the Gobi desert. It was just... horrible. The locals call them 'haboobs' which means 'blown'."

Tom watched the swirling storm apprehensively. It was very far away but Tom could imagine its devastating effects. Fear glimmered in his eyes. Hawk noticed his distress and tried to reassure him. "That storm looks really far away. We would be the most unluckiest people on Earth if we get hit by that beast. It is really dark, as well. Maybe our eyes are just messing with us. You can't tell."

"Yeah. You can't tell. The next thing you know we're in the middle of another Godzilla." He was referring to one of the most famous events linked to the Sahara desert. In June

Abir Gupta

2020, a "Godzilla" dust plume travelled from the Sahara, across the Atlantic ocean to North America which degraded the air quality in the Caribbean Basin. "That storm isn't our problem right now. Our problem is getting to the base. Come on."

The storm set the mood for the next couple of hours until they decided to take a longer break in which they could eat food. Hawk laid out the silk mat and handed Tom the clump of dates to snack on. They were bitter but full of fructose."We're burning through these quicker than I thought. Not very filling, either. Suddenly, Hawk had grabbed Tom's arm. "Pass me the knife! Quick!" Without questioning his strange behaviour, Tom handed him the blade. Hawk already had his pole in his hand and was jabbing it into the sand, crawling frantically around stabbing the knife into the sand. For a second, Tom thought his friend had gone crazy until he returned with something on the end of the knife. "Is that a fish?" Tom asked. Hawk shook his head, looking for the fire-making equipment. "A sandfish. It's actually not a fish." Tom was perplexed. There was a fish in the middle of the desert? "Where is the water?" he asked.

"Unfortunately, there's no water. Though I'm thinking there might be something nearby." He held up the 20-centimeter black-and-yellow striped reptile. "These are actually okay to eat- they're harmless. People have done it before. Can you get a fire going?" Tom started building a fire using the seat fluff. There was a small portion of wood left over from the previous fire so Tom didn't need to resort to using his clothes.

After Hawk had finished with the sandfish, he set up a splint and skewered the meat. "This will be quite the feast!" he joked optimistically. "And we still have all the tuna left over." After the sandfish was finished roasting in the fire's heat, Tom and Hawk started their meal. The stew had all but finished and Tom had to agree sandfish didn't have the same taste as turkey. Through a mouthful of sandfish, Hawk said, "I was wondering where the sandfish came from. Water must be quite close. There could be a pothole nearby which has collected water over the years. Look out for a bush or tree- they're the reason water doesn't evaporate in some potholes." Tom nodded, too tired to talk. He had spotted some forms of plant life but all of them were dead and too skimpy to stop any water from evaporating.

After eating, Tom and Hawk packed up the picnic and instead of picking up the trail again, Hawk made a decision. "We should rest for a little bit here. You look quite tired and I am too. If we get a short nap, then we can go on for the whole night without needing long breaks. What do you say?" Tom was more than happy to sleep and agreed eagerly. "Can you set a thirty-minute timer while I get the sleeping bag ready?" Hawk asked Tom. His mouth was full of water so Tom just nodded and fiddled with his watch while Hawk unpacked the sleeping bag and laid it out on a roll mat to ensure a comfortable sleep. "Hey, there's only one sleeping bag!" Tom pointed out. Hawk responded by pulling out a large blanket which was dotted with various badges. Tom noticed the purple Scouting insignia stitched onto the middle of the blanket. "I'll sleep under the stars, if you don't mind." Hawk caught Tom's gaze as he analyzed the blanket. "This is my Scout blanket. I joined up when I was young and when my uniform didn't have any space for badges, my mother would sew them onto this blanket. It's special."

Without another word, Hawk settled back in his blanket and within seconds, his eyes were closed. Tom could tell from the sound of his breathing that the man had fallen asleep. Tom slid into the sleeping bag. It was pitch black and the only source of light was the moon. He took a lot longer to fall asleep than Hawk. Tom watched the embers from the remains of the fire dancing high into the sky before burning out and falling to the ground as ashes. Tom watched until the last ember died out before finally falling asleep.

Chapter 18

Crunch! The Jeep ploughed into the ruins of the fire, ash exploding into the sky. Chunks of charred wood littered the floor as the smugglers steeped out of the car, guns at the ready. Tom was jolted from his sleep, groggily staring around. A dream? He heard angry shouts and saw a shimmer of red shoot into the sky. It was a flare. Tom was on his feet immediately, whipping his head around as the smuggler closed in on him. Somehow they had found him. Tom still couldn't believe he was in reality; this couldn't be happening.

Tom came to his senses as an indistinguishable, silhouetted figure rose behind the five men ganging up on him. The first shot fired from the gun sounded like a crack from a whip. The alarmed men turned around only to find Hawk standing heroically, gun in hand. A smuggler sprawled on the floor had taken a shot on the shoulder, not lethal but the damage had been done. *One less danger to worry about*, Hawk thought as Ferdinand clutched his shoulder in agony, screaming. The four remaining men abruptly took action, firing their guns. Hawk threw himself to the floor as the night sky was ripped apart.

Tom had been frozen on the spot until Hawk bellowed a single word at him. "Run!" For no reason, Tom grabbed his roll mat before he turned and sprinted away into the night. Unfortunately, someone had noticed him and was already taking aim. Tom felt bullets graze against him as he ran, his heart racing along with his brain. One break had led to no less than five smugglers locating them, possibly more coming after the flare had been fired. Tom saw Hawk burst from the ruins of the camp, limping on his stick as he was shot at. Tom watched with horror as Hawk crumpled to the floor. He couldn't believe what he was seeing. He watched as the group of smugglers swarmed over him, one of them watching for signs of movement while another listened for the sound of breathing.

In an instant, they had decided. The man was not going to stand again. But where was his accomplice? All of them turned their attention to the small figure standing like a statue, watching them. Tom was petrified and only turned to run when the first few shots were fired at him. He felt numb with grief. Hawk was...gone. They hadn't known each other too well but Tom felt a wave of sadness crash over him. Once again, he was alone. But fear powered him on, the motivation that if he kept running, he could have a chance of surviving and seeing his father again, kept him alive. But motivation would only get him so far. He was in plain sight, even in the darkness and needed to switch up the game play.

Tom had the advantage because he had gotten a headstart while the smugglers had only just begun chasing him. He was smaller than them and had a better chance of hiding so that was another plus. Apart from that, Tom couldn't see any other pros he had, being a fourteen-year old being chased by four fully-grown men armed with machine guns.

Tom darted to the left, where a dune stood. Of course, the smugglers noticed this movement and tried to follow Tom up the dune. He had scrambled up at light speed even with the mat, something he wouldn't have dared doing because he could get injured. But this was different.

Tom had purposefully led the men onto the dune to slow them down. It was obvious they didn't have much experience climbing them when they had a Jeep. The men stumbled, falling flat on their faces. One of them tried to fire at Tom but the shot went wild as he too slipped. Tom smiled to himself. It would take them precious time to work the dune out and by then, he would have disappeared. Still, he had to get down the dune first. Then Tom realised why he had brought the mat with him. Not only did it save many bullets from hitting him but it doubled as a sled. Without taking time to tell himself how stupid the idea was, Tom threw it onto the floor and lay down on the makeshift getaway sled.

Tom felt himself beginning to move as the roll mat began its descent. The smooth material caused little to no friction as Tom speedily zipped down the dune. He felt like shouting out with excitement. The mat began to pick up speed and Tom felt his stomach churn. Tom noticed the rock sticking out from the dune a millisecond too late and felt himself thrown from the mat as it was uprooted by the small rock. Tom felt his bones jar as he was carelessly slammed against the ground. He rolled a few meters before coming to a stop on the other side of the dune

Everything hurt. In pain, Tom stood up, craning his neck upwards. He stared with amazement. He couldn't believe he had skidded down the dune in seconds. A rock, similar in size to the one that had left him with a twisted ankle, had nearly killed him as he had been launched into the air. But Tom couldn't worry about a sore back now. The smugglers were still coming. Leaving the bullet-ridden roll mat in the dust, Tom ran as fast as his bruised legs would carry him. In the space of a few minutes, he had sustained many wounds both from the descent down the dune and from the bullets that had skimmed him.

Tom heard his feet pound against the floor as he sprinted on. Sweat poured down his face, mixing with tears of sorrow which he didn't realise had been shed. Tom continued for the next minute, racing along the desert for until his lungs were screaming for him to stop. Tom decelerated and finally came to a stop, gratefully heaving in oxygen from the air. The dune was far away now, mixing in with the others that dotted the Sahara. He was almost certain that the smugglers weren't following him now. Why would they care to chase a helpless boy who would probably be killed off by starvation or thirst?

Tom knew he couldn't fall asleep now. He had to be alert for any smugglers who had changed their minds. For the next three-quarters of an hour, Tom was spread out on the sand, one eye open for danger. He had a terrible headache. Too much had happened in so little time. Tom was huddled in a ball, trying not to fall asleep. Hawk. He was presumably still lying there. Tom had to get back to the camp. There was no doubt they had demolished everything but Tom still had to go back there- not that there would be much left. Tom remembered how the bullets had completely trashed the camp. Nothing would have been spared.

Finally, Tom decided to go back. There was no point in just lying there, waiting for the sun to roast him alive. And so Tom spent the next hour navigating his way back to the camp. In the distance, Tom heard a vehicle speeding off into the night. The smugglers had finally left. They had left behind a scene of wreckage and destruction, changing everything for Tom.

The camp came into distance. But Tom wasn't interested in it. He was looking for Hawk. Tom remembered the spot where the smugglers, with their horrible guns firing numerous darts of death, had taken out Hawk. But he wasn't there. Tom searched around for any signs of the man but there was nothing. That was it. For whatever reason, the smugglers had taken Hawk with them. There was nothing Tom could do. He returned to the camp. Ash had been sprayed everywhere, coating the dark green sleeping bag. Tom brushed the sleeping bag down, stuffing it into its bag. Tom found his holed bag lying under a piece of charred wood. Tom kicked it aside and seized the bag. It still had everything in it. But why was it so wet?

The water. Tom unzipped his bag to find the water soaking into the lining, the bottle smashed to pieces by the barrage of bullets. No water. His second bottle, luckily, was lying amongst the ashes, unharmed. But there was only a few mouthfuls left in it. Strangely, Tom noticed that Hawk's bag was missing. The smugglers appeared to have taken Hawk and his things. Now all Tom was left with was a small amount of water, his pocket knife, the bunch of dates and whatever items in his rucksack that had survived. His situation had just gotten worse. Tom couldn't take any more. He threw himself onto the floor, rocking back and forth. He was lost. There was no hope.

Worse still, It was nearly morning. Tom saw fragments of the sun shining through the dark layer of clouds. "No, no!" Tom had no shelter as it had been in Hawk's back. Luckily, the silk sheet still remained along with some suitable firewood he could use to cook up a shelter, like he had on his second day in the Sahara. Realising there was no point in sulking, Tom began hastily throwing things into his rucksack. He hoped his meagre supply of things could help him survive long enough to reach ISIO's base. However, Tom knew it wasn't possible. Something had to happen. A miracle. Otherwise it was unlikely Tom would ever get out of the desert.

Tom began the hike, continuing on the perilous journey forwards. Before setting up camp, Tom wanted to get as far away from the scene of wreckage as he could. He never knew when the smugglers would decide to come back for him. Tom almost didn't have the willpower to move on. What was the point? Then he saw something. What was that in the distance? A small speck. It was moving. Tom tried to work out whether it was getting closer to him or further away. It might just have been the smugglers in their Jeep but they would have gotten a lot further away in the time since they had left.

Anyhow, Tom had to investigate. This was his big opportunity. He had no other choice, really. He could go there and find the smugglers. Or he could go there and find something else, something that could save him from his predicament. Tom was aware of the sun which was growing stronger. Already he felt its heat. Before leaving, Tom went up to the remains of the fire and picked up a burned lump of wood before smearing the charcoal from it onto his fingers. He applied the charcoal to his face, leaving streaks of black protecting his face from the sun. It was a handy trick his father had taught him. He had said if there were the next best thing to sunscreen or a pair of sunglasses.

They were just the thing he needed. While he would hopefully be out in the sun for a short time, they would come in handy and stop him from becoming a roast dinner for any animals who happened to wander by. After fully painting his face in charcoal, Tom was ready. It was time to go.

Tom still had no idea if the spot had been a mirage or something that could save his life. It was a big gamble but Tom had decided. He was at the stage where some risks had to be taken otherwise he would perish. The Sahara would never be a forgiving place. Tom forced himself to pick up his pace, not so fast he would sweat and lose salt but not allowing himself to be in the sun too long. After some time of purposeful hiking, Tom was almost certain the growing speck was heading towards him. It was too small to be anything like a Jeep and was more likely to be an animal.

The sun was dominant over the skies once again. Tom felt himself roasting and remembered to wrap the silk over himself. Tom had noticed that the ground ahead of him flattening out. There were no more dunes. Was it a good sign? Tom felt the ground harden underneath him. Tom felt his spirits lift as the daunting thought of climbing another dune was left behind him, buried in the sand. It was only after a few minutes of celebration that Tom realised what exactly he was standing on. A salt pan. The sea had been here once and the salt and minerals had been left behind after the water evaporated. The result was a solid crust of sodium chloride concealing quagmires of mud which could engulf whole trucks, and, as Tom dreamed, whole Jeeps as well. Along with anyone inside.

Another negative was that no plants grew here. There was no chance of finding water. And the Tarahumara trick just wouldn't do it forever. Tom was not dissuaded, however. He just knew whatever he was heading to was good. After all that bad, how could there not be good?

It started to come into view. Tom squinted in the harsh sunlight, making out the camel. It was a large, hairy creature with humps which stored fat which the creature could later metabolize. It had thin legs that looked like they would collapse at any moment and a big-lipped snout. Tom had heard that a camel could survive for over two weeks without water. It was a wondrous creature with no known predators, apart from wild dogs or dingoes who could take the young. But this was a beautiful, fully-grown camel. And standing next to it was a man.

Tom stumbled forwards. A man who wasn't a smuggler or agent. Then Tom reeled forwards, his head spinning. He was baking. The heat was just too intense. Tom tried to reach out to the man but was too dizzy. His eyelids shut and he slumped to the floor.

Chapter 19

Tom awoke, staring at a roof of a tent. He was not in the sun but turned to look outside. It was the middle of the day outside. Tom felt a sharp pain in his head and closed his eyes, settling back on the cotton quilt laid out for him. Where was he? There was a small ceramic cup on the sand next to Tom. He was parched and slowly sipped on the water while examining his surroundings. The tent he was in appeared to be made of some sort of animal pelt, goat perhaps.

Tom tried to move but each time he did parts of him erupted in pain. His back had been injured during the stunt down the dune and his legs and arms were grazed from the bullets. Somebody had applied bandages to him and his wounds disappeared beneath the protective wrapping. Along with the cup of water, someone had left him a meal. There was a plate of cooked vegetables with rice and some chicken skewers on the side. Tom began to rip into the meat, wolfing down the meal to restore his health faster.

After eating his fill, Tom had reenergized. He had enough strength to stand up, to try to recall what had happened. There was a camel with a man standing next to it. Tom had tried to reach it but had fainted in the heat. After that... Tom had no idea what had happened and who brought him here. Tom decided to find the man with the camel and started walking to the doorway of light. But just then, somebody walked into the tent. He was a short, bearded man wearing a black robe, a sleeveless cloak and a traditional headcloth. Black robes gained two to three times as much heat by radiation from the Sun as white robes, but enhanced convection of air beneath the robe carried that heat away before it reached the skin.

The man, presumably the one who owned the camel, led Tom back to his cotton quilt which he had been lying on. Tom felt blessed to be connected with civilisation once again. Tom kneeled on his quilt, waiting for the man to speak. When he uttered his first word it was obvious he did not know how to speak English very well. Tom noticed his heavy Berber accent and realised he was an Amazigh, an indigenous tribe who flourished in Northern Africa across Morocco, Algeria and Libya. The French's colonial legacy had left parts of Northern Africa able to speak their language and this Berber tribe could very fluently speak French.

"I Amastan," the Amazigh man began. "I bring you to safe place" He indicated around the tent. In his hand was a chipped bowl engraved with elegant designs. "I bring you green tea. Drink." He held out the bowl and Tom took it from him, gently blowing on the tea before sipping it and savouring its rich flavours. As Tom drank, Amastan told him his story. He had been out searching for an oasis that had been spotted when he had seen Tom. He had fainted and the camel had carried him back to the village. Tom knew how to speak a little bit of broken French and replied, "Merci, Amastan." The Amazigh grinned with recognition and watched Tom drink the tea until he had finished, handing back the bowl.

"Je M'appelle Tom. Where am I?" Tom spoke a mixture of French and English hoping Amastan would understand some of it. In response to Tom's question, he spread his arms wide and said, "Home." Tom looked at him quizzically, beckoning Amastan to tell him more. He stood up and signalled Tom to follow him. Tom obliged and was led outside where he got his first look of what Amastan called Home. The village was small, based around a rocky outcrop. Some houses were made of red clay bricks that had been dried in the sun while others were built from pise, a building material of stiff earth.

At first, Tom thought the village was deserted but then noticed the small children climbing up and down the outcrop, laughing and shouting. Tom was amazed at how effortlessly they could climb- the Berber children were as sure-footed as a mountain goat. Indeed, there was a woman in a black dress tending to a herd of black goats while another man was shearing one with an iron tool of some sort. Goats were vital for dairy and their fur was a useful clothing item.

Tethered to the tent with a thick rope was the camel which Tom had seen earlier. It bleated as it recognized Tom. Amastan gestured towards the camel. "Camel take you here. Save you." Tom stroked the camels fur, running his hands up and down its humps. Tom noticed a young girl running up to the camel, placing a bucket of yellowing grass at its feet. She shyly glanced at Tom before slipping away to join her friends.

Amastan was staring at the Atlas mountains which Tom detected were much, much closer than the last time he had seen them. "I maybe take you to mountain. More people live there who help lost ones." Tom nodded before returning to the tent to escape the heat but Amastan grabbed his shirt to stop him. Inside the tent, there were two men similarly dressed to Amastan who were jabbing at the sand with their sticks. "Serpent."

Tom translated that to snake. The men were snake-hunting and they had found one by the look of it. Tom backed away from the tent, not looking forward to any more deadly snake encounters. A thin smile spread across Amastan's face. "It will not hurt you. Come, you need rest." Tom obediently followed him into a small clay house, the walls cracked and needing repair. Inside, there was a woman cooking. The aroma of meat filled the house.

Tom didn't have time to admire the ornaments adorning the room before he was taken into a smaller space around the size of a broomstick cupboard. Again, there was a quilt waiting for him. Tom removed his boots and took the opportunity to relax. Meanwhile, Amastan talked to the lady in an incomprehensible spit of words. The lady nodded and glimpsed the exhausted boy laying on the quilt and started filling a cracked pot with water for him to drink. Amastan returned to Tom and whispered, "You safe now. Sleep." Tom was already slumbering.

***

"It's here."

The Jeep's door violently slammed shut as the five men, one with a bandaged shoulder stepped out of the car. "They must be hiding them in this village." The driver of the Jeep said. "I've had enough of ISIO. We are Desert Ghost and nothing can stand in our way. We'll report back once the vermin have been eliminated. Some extra cash won't hurt. The other smugglers grinned wickedly. "Bonjour!" A voice behind them spoke. The smugglers turned around to find themselves face to face with a Berber. Without responding, the smugglers elbowed their way past into the main settlement.

Tom awoke suddenly. His heart was racing. He had heard the strange movement outside and on cue, Amastan ran into the house. Without a word, he threw thick blanket over Tom. "No move!" He said. Tom was rigid with fear. He had an inkling as to who had found him. Through a crack in the wall, Tom could see all the commotion happening outside. His worse fears had come true. They were back. Tom was certain that Desert Ghost had some sort of aerial transportation that was reporting everything that wasn't desert. How else could they have found the camp or village?

A strong-looking, young man strode forward angrily with a pole. He was the same snake-hunter Tom had seen earlier. But one of the smugglers waved his gun at the man, pointing at the stick and then the ground. The hunter dropped his stick before slowly backing away. Tom knew who they were here for. The whole village was in danger. Mothers were gathering their children and taking them inside, barring the door of their houses shut. The men of the village were watching the smugglers ransack their homes. They were clearly looking for something but what? They had left all the jewellery and food. What more could they want?

The smugglers hadn't hurt anyone yet but Tom knew it was only a matter of time before the situation would get sticky. They were ruthless and Tom knew they could hurt anyone at anytime. If Tom didn't show himself, than the village was at the mercy of Desert Ghost. As much as Tom wanted to stay hidden and safe in his little corner of the house, he knew he had to do something.

That's it, Tom told himself. He threw off the blanket and gallantly walked out of the house. People watched the newcomer as he shouted out to the men invading their village. "Desert Ghost! Leave the Amazighs alone! Take me and leave them." The group of men turned to see the same child who had escaped from them lividly striding up to them. One of the smugglers nudged another. "It's a child. The one working with ISIO. You think the boss will want him alive? We can find out what ISIO wants with a child like him."

The driver nodded in response. "Fine. But he's your duty." The smuggler went out to meet Tom. Not scared, Tom stared into his eyes that were alit with hatred. He roughly grabbed hold of his wrists and dragged him over to his colleagues. The Amazighs watched as their guest was dragged away. Amastan took as step forward, ready to save Tom but the Jeep driver waved him back, looking threatening with his gun. Tom gave the villagers an encouraging smile that told them everything would be alright but deep inside Tom wasn't so sure.

One of the smugglers went over to the tethered camel, Amastan nervously watching. He pulled out a knife and for a horrible second Tom thought he was going to harm the camel. But instead he slashed the rope, freeing the camel. The smuggler came back with a piece of rope in his hands. He grabbed Tom's wrists, wrapping the rope around them very tightly. Tom could feel his blood circulation cut off and wiggled his hands inconspicuously, trying to loosen the rope.

Amastan boldly walked over to his camel, stroking its face before gently leading it inside a house. He was gone. Tom couldn't believe he had turned himself in as he was roughly shoved across the village towards the Jeep. He was slammed against the door and then pushed inside the car. The driver and the man who had bind Tom's wrists together were sitting at the front of the car while he, Ferdinand and the other two smugglers piled up in the back.

Tom was uncomfortably squashed against the door, with the all the smugglers shooting him dirty looks. The driver started the engine, the Jeep roaring into life. Tom took one last look at the village. All the children and woman had gone inside, only the men still holding their sticks anxiously watching. The Jeep started driving away from the village. He was in captivity.

Tom tried to get some sleep on the journey but each time they bumped on a rock his head went shooting into the framework above him. It made it even harder to sleep when he had a paining head. On top of that, it was too dangerous to fall asleep surrounded by smugglers. What if they tried to hurt him? But Tom told himself that if they had wanted to hurt him, they would have done it when he turned himself in and they wanted him alive for some reason. That was a plus. Tom tried to remember the landscape and the different landmarks dotted around the desert so he could try to work out how to get back to the village if he ever escaped from custody.

With nothing else to do, Tom tried to spark up a conversation which would give him a bit more insight. "Um, where are we going?" His confidence had disappeared. The other smugglers growled at him. "Another word," The driver hissed. "And I'll toss you into the desert and leave you for the birds." For a second, Tom wondered if he should take up the offer. But he had less of a chance of survival with no supplies whatsoever than if he went with the smugglers. Another bonus was it was possible Tom would be led straight to his father. Tom told himself to just hold on a little longer. They had been driving for hours and it wouldn't be long before they reached their destination.

Abir Gupta

Tom unsurprisingly hadn't been offered refreshments or snacks but was too scared to ask for some. If he did, then it was very possible he would become the snack for any passing animal. Things weren't looking too good for him. As Tom shifted his legs to get into a more comfortable position, they brushed against something. A crate. This was what they were smuggling! Tom was the closest to the crate, Ferdinand next to him supposedly guarding it while all he was doing was snoring. Tom knew this was his golden opportunity. He nudged the crate with his toe. It didn't move. Something heavy was inside it.

Tom was about to investigate further when he heard a small pop beneath him. The driver shouted in frustration. He was glaring at Tom as if he was responsible. The driver climbed out of the Jeep, crouching low by one of the tires. "A puncture!" He screamed. "Somebody left a nail in the middle of the desert! How come none of you saw it, huh?" The five people sitting in the Jeep didn't respond. The driver growled. Tom saw his hand inch towards the pistol in his holster but then he said, "Fine. We're going on foot. It's not far. Now don't you dare drop the crate..."

Hands still bound together, Tom was propelled forward as the driver pushed him. He spun to the floor, scrambling back up as fast as he could. The six of them started the short journey to wherever the smugglers wanted to go. Tom watched as Ferdinand hauled the crate out of the truck, lugging it along with him. He just needed a distraction to break into it...

It came into view. A helicopter, shining and brand new. It was a CH-47 Chinook, one of the most iconic helicopters in the world. It was a military transport helicopter standing right in front of them. To Tom, its presence was more overwhelming than the Blackhawk. "This is it, boys. We'll get to the airstrip in another hour, tops. Get in." Tom thought about what the driver had just said. An airstrip? What was this about?

With all those thoughts whirling around in his head, Tom climbed into the Chinook, followed by the other men. Ferdinand came last, hauling the crate into the helicopter. The driver and another man disappeared into the cockpit area while Ferdinand and the other two smugglers stayed behind with Tom in the seating compartment. The crate was placed at the back of the helicopter.

Tom sat down on the seat on the edge of the row of seats while the other three men sat side by side on the other end of the row of seats. Nobody was watching over Tom but there was no need to. He was tied up and was harmless. Much sooner than Tom thought, the helicopter began rising into the air. From what he knew, he only had an hour before they reached the airstrip- where there were bound to be more smugglers. He needed a plan.

The Chinook took off into the night sky, the doors automatically sliding shut. Bright lights came on inside the helicopter and Tom could now look around for anything that could help him. There were no visible parachutes which would make getting of the helicopter much harder but Tom would deal with that problem after figuring out how to get rid of the rope. With it still tied around his wrists, he would be unable to do anything with falling flat on the floor.

The seat buckle! Tom could use that to cut away at the rope and then he would be free. It was worth a shot. Tom leant over and began sawing away.

Chapter 20

Tom's wrists were scraped and bleeding. He had been at it for almost twenty minutes. He had estimated the time because before take off the smugglers had removed his watch and anything else that could be an aid to him. The rope was unfortunately very thick and the seat buckle was blunt. Still, it was working. Tom cut away at the rope, digging the buckle deeper into it with each movement back and forth.

And then it came off. It simply fell away from Tom's wrists. He made sure not to get too excited and arouse suspicion among the men just meters away from him. Tom took a few seconds to rub his wrists. They were stinging badly. But he was finally free!

Tom's mind raced, trying to figure out his next move. He had to reach the crate and find out what was in it. He was very close to it and if Tom was quiet enough, then he could reach it without being spotted. Tom was about to move before the Chinook started shaking violently. The other smugglers didn't seem to be fazed, however. Tom sighed with relief as he realised it was just some turbulence. Tom continued sneaking his way to the crate like a ninja. It was right there... the source of all this trouble.

Tom crouched down and slowly started sliding off the lid. His hands were sweaty. He didn't know what he was going to find. He took a deep breath and lifted up the lid. He looked into the crate. Nestled amongst foam blocks was... wine? What? Tom was shocked. All of that trouble just to smuggle some wine? But Tom got the impression that it was part of a bigger picture. All of this couldn't be because they wanted to have a giant party. There was something else. Then a voice shouted, "Hey!"

Tom turned around. Ferdinand had gotten up to stretch his legs, spotting the boy with the wine bottle in his hands. "He's got the crate!" The other two men stood up, pulling out there guns. At the same time, the man who had been sitting with the pilot had burst out of the cockpit, shouting. "Something's been spotted on the radar. ISIO- they've found us!" Tom smiled. He silently whooped to himself. But it wasn't over yet. Tom dived behind one of the seats as the men started shooting. Bullets embedded themselves in the crate, splinters flying everywhere.

The wine bottle in Tom's hand smashed, liquid and glass all over the floor. The smugglers were about to fire again, but they dropped their guns as an explosion occurred outside. The Chinook was quivered. Tom saw one of the windows covered with a thick screen of smoke. "We've been hit!" Ferdinand screamed as he ducked for cover. The men weren't interested in the annoying boy anymore. They were only interested in their survival. Tom heard the pilot shout, "We have your man!" even though there was no chance of him being heard.

This was the moment. Tom darted to the back of the Chinook where the exit hatch was. Soldiers used the ramp to board the Chinook and that was how Tom would escape. There was a red button on the wall, its paint flaky. Tom knew if he didn't escape the helicopter, he would go down with the rest of them. Behind him, the smugglers were screaming like children, running around with no idea what to do. They were helpless.

Tom brought his hand down on the button, the hatch opening. He grabbed onto the rail so he wouldn't fly out of the helicopter. The smugglers had locked themselves in the cockpit area, trying to evade the hail of bullets smashing through the windows. Tom's hair whipped everywhere in the wind and it took all his strength to not fly out of the Chinook. The attacking helicopter came into view. It was another Blackhawk, similar to the one that had taken Jacob Flashfire.

Tom's eyes teared up in the wind again. In the cockpit, he saw familiar ISIO agents. They were staring at him with amazement. For one millisecond, everything seemed to slow down. The pilot couldn't believe Tom was still alive, nor could the other man standing in the cockpit. It was Hawk. Tom almost couldn't believe what he was seeing. He was so, so happy that Hawk was alive! The agent had somehow saved himself!

Tom noticed the flurry of activity in the cockpit as a rope was released from the bottom of the helicopter. Tom's jaw dropped. "No." He said to himself. "I can't do this." Tom had to make a move. The Chinook was losing altitude and it wouldn't be long before it ended up like the Bell 212. Tom saw the small figures in the cockpit screaming at him and even thought Tom couldn't hear them, he knew they were telling him to jump. Another few seconds and the rope would be completely out of range. *You can do this!* Tom fixed his eyes on the dangling rope, his knees bent. Then he jumped.

Tom was flying through the air, leaving the Chinook beneath him. His hand reached out to grab the rope... and he was on! Tom was holding onto the rope with both hands so tight his knuckles were going pale. He was getting tossed around in the wind and he didn't know if he had the strength to pull himself up. He didn't have a choice. Tom started heaving himself up, ignoring his screaming muscles as he inched towards safety. He was so close.

A hand reached out to him. Hawk showed his head, shouting, "Hold on!" Tom gripped his hand tightly, the other still holding onto the rope as he was pulled up. Hawk lifted him into the Blackhawk. He was safe. Both of them lay on the cold metal floor, heaving for air. After Tom had finished panting, he said, "Hawk! How are you alive?" Hawk responded by flitting back into the cockpit, slamming down on another button which sent a second missile soaring through the air. It barely missed the Chinook, exploding above it, taking out the main rotor.

"They're finished. But we're not too high so they'll probably be alright." Hawks said, from his seat next to the pilot. Tom didn't care. He was still shocked Hawk was alive. "How are you-"

"How am I still alive?" Hawk flashed Tom a smile. "It looked like they shot me down but guess what? I was wearing a bullet-proof vest. It's an essential. They didn't know that, though, so I played dead." Tom couldn't believe Hawk had tricked them. It made sense how Hawk's bag wasn't there. "After that, Marcus right here picked me up. I couldn't find you so I assumed the smugglers had taken you. I guess I was right?" Tom shook his head.

"It's kind of a long story. So there was this camel..." Tom narrated his story to Hawk, telling him how he had turned himself in to protect the village. "That was very brave of you, Tom. I'm sure they're all grateful to you. But wine? That's strange. Something's up." From behind them, the experienced pilot started speaking into the intercom."I've been tracking them for a while. It looks like they were heading to the old airstrip."

Tom looked at Hawk quizzically. "The old airstrip was used by aerial fire-fighters. It had planes, helicopters... that sort of thing. They used the airstrip to stop fires across Northern Africa until they were offered another, better airstrip in Rabat. Apparently, they left all the vehicles there. Keys, maintenance trucks, the whole lot is still there. They must have needed them for something." The intercom crackled as the pilot spoke again. "It's possible that all the smugglers are headed there so I have sent out a signal. The other units should know and they'll be on their way."

"And what about us?" Tom asked. He was always ready for more action if it meant seeing his father. "We're sitting this one out." Hawk said. "My leg hasn't healed and I'm not going to send you out there again. We would be on our way home but we volunteered as a backup vehicle so we're going to the airstrip. But we'll be up in the sky, safe and sound. Congrats! You made it through your first mission." Tom was flabbergasted. "What? But I want to go down there and help!" He couldn't just sit back up here while everyone would be fighting! "Sorry, Tom. Ms Challaby wouldn't want you to do this either. Trust me, we've deployed everything from the military base so these smugglers won't stand a chance."

***

The man who Tom knew as Bulk was pouring over a sheet of paper, re-explaining the plan to his men. The planes were almost fully prepared outside. Bulk was inside what used to be the lounge. The aerial fire-fighters' living quarters had been knocked down to create an above-ground bunker with an armoury inside. The homely atmosphere created by the bean bags, tables with playing cards spread over them, a plasma television, a coffee machine and fridge stocked with snacks had been wrecked by the cold, unwelcoming tone in the renovated airstrip.

"Listen up! Get over here!" Bulk shouted. The identically dressed smugglers milling around the room immediately headed over to the low, rectangular table where a map of London was spread out. "You know the plan. But I don't want anyone messing up so I'm gonna go over it one last time." The smugglers pretended to look interested as they heard the master plan for the tenth time. "So, when the rest of you get here with the wine, we load up the tanks. Then, we attach them to the vehicles and get to London. Easy so far, right? Then you know all of your allocated flight routes where you'll spray the alcohol over London. Then, we'll send a little spark and ISIO will have gone up in flames." He started manically laughing.

The other smugglers thought their leader was crazy. He was kindling such a hatred for ISIO he would burn down the whole of London with wine? But they had learned to not question his weird and wonderful methods. They had worked before, and they had been paid a lot of money. It would work again and they would be paid a lot of money. Who were they to argue with?

"Sir," One of the smugglers tentatively started speaking. Bulk turned to face him with his cold black eyes. "Royce? What is it?" Somehow, he could tell each man apart even when they were dressed identically. "What do you want us to do with the man you captured?" Bulk laughed again. It gave him power to think that Jacob Flashfire was at his mercy. "He's told me the whereabouts of ISIO. I don't think we need him anymore. We have no time to muck about with him. Go start fuelling the planes. Benny, give a call to the others. When will those useless smugglers speed up?" He left the room in a grumpy mood. He was really just anxious about the operation. He understood the consequences of being caught. Yet for years he had managed to evade his enemy. What could go wrong?

Abir Gupta

Outside, the red-and-white striped planes were being fuelled. More Jeeps entered the compound, men transporting crates chocked with wine bottles. The recently repainted airstrip was gleaming in the harsh sunlight. Bulk was watching his men labour from inside the air-conditioned weapons room while men buzzed around him choosing their arms. Men had already started preparing the helitanks, filling them with the wine they had smuggled across Africa.

The dull brick building was the first thing that came into view. The Bell AH-1Z Viper, a sleek attack helicopter, was inching into the scene. The C-unit, who specialised in air-to-ground assaults, were the first unit to arrive at the pinpointed location given to them by the Blackhawk's pilot. Trailing behind them was another similar helicopter which was transporting the three members of the B-unit who had split up with Hawk. ISIO had lost contact with the A-unit but the B, C, D, E and F unit, along with a couple of backup units were all on their way to the abandoned airstrip.

Earlier that day, the Viper had intercepted a phone call, using the advanced technology ISIO's scientists had designed for them. It was smuggler-to-smuggler, and while they hadn't managed to put a stop to any of the various parties spread out across the Sahara, the phone call was the key to success. The motive behind smuggling thousands of bottles of wine, or so they had been told, was revealed in the space of a minute. It was simply ludicrous. Many agents believed Desert Ghost had been bluffing and it was intended for them to intercept the call, and then Desert

Ghost would maybe lie about their location to buy some time or play some elaborate trick on them. But the call had been traced back to the abandoned airstrip which was the location they had been given by the pilot.

As the airstrip came into clear view, they knew at once that it wasn't a bluff. Large tanks were being filled with liquid which was presumably the large quantities of wine they had smuggled. Wine smuggling wasn't uncommon, but to use it in the way Desert Ghost was had never been seen before. They were so unpredictable; that was what made them so dangerous. The pilot had decided to inform all the other units of their plan.

Tom saw the numerous helicopters join emerge from the clouds. They had got the call. Many models of military helicopters, both transport and attack, had assembled above the airstrip. Through the tinted glass of each helicopter, Tom couldn't distinguish the different units but all that mattered was that they were all there. "Did you hear their plan? It's absurd!" Hawk said to Tom, exasperated.

"I know. It's pretty crazy but will it work?" Tom replied. Hawk shook his head. "I don't know. Even if it doesn't, they've got millions of pounds of wine with them." There was no further conversation. Both of them went back to what they were doing before. "Hawk?"

"Tom?" Hawk looked up from the controls he had been examining.

"What's our battle plan? I mean, will they just charge in there?" Tom asked. Everything had been going good and well until then. Now doubts began to arise within Tom as he got more and more nervous. He knew he would be safe up in the helicopter but he couldn't shake off the feeling that something bad was going to happen. "They already know we're here. The clouds have given us some cover but those aerial fire-fighters had top-notch equipment. Their radars have probably picked us up."

"That's comforting." Tom replied. From the grimy window, he saw the first helicopter starting to descend. Men were poised, parachutes double-checked. ISIO were the first to strike. The Viper's three-barrelled rotary canon spun into life, raining its darts of death upon the airstrip. Desert Ghost responded immediately and one of the tiny figures on the ground calmly headed towards an artillery gun which had been installed to stop any intruders after the fire-fighters had left. The moment the artillery started firing the Blackhawk's pilot jerked the joystick upwards and the helicopter disappeared into the clouds.

"Aim for the tanks!" The message was broadcasted to each helicopter. With bulletproof glass and metal armour, the artillery gun didn't do much damage to the helicopters but made it impossible for any agents to parachute out. The bullets were sent ricocheting of the helicopters, littering the floor. "We're out of ammo!" Somebody on the ground shouted as the gun stopped firing. ISIO took the opportunity and suddenly the sky was a mass of bright colours as half the men descended into the battle.

Desert Ghost was quick to respond and within minutes every man had a weapon. The machine guns, however, didn't have enough precision. to hit any of the agents who were nearing the ground quickly. But that gave the smugglers an advantages. The first bullets pierced through one parachute and the man attached to it was falling. The sagging bundle of silk crashed to the floor with him. Luckily, he had been close to the ground so didn't sustain any major injuries. The captain of the C-unit threw himself to the ground, firing relentlessly at the smugglers until the other agents joined him. ISIO wasn't the army; mainly, it was spying and collecting data. But sometimes, things were a little bit different.

The men who had been expecting to fly down with tasers or handcuffs were surprised. Instead, they had landed on the roof of the weapons building with their rifles and were firing away. The battle had been split into three parts. Riflemen sniping each other down from behind crates or trucks, ducking and dodging. Then there was the main battle raging on the airstrip as ISIO agents tried to shoot out the tanks of wine while Desert Ghost smugglers held them back. The last part of the battle was taking place inside the building, where a unit of agents had busted in to try and find Jacob Flashfire.

One of the riflemen's shots went wild as he ducked down to avoid a bullet. His shot exploded into the wine tank, glass and liquid spraying everywhere. Agents and smugglers alike shielded their heads and fled to avoid the sharp glass flying everywhere. The wine was seeping into the ground, wasted. But Desert Ghost still had enough to raze London to the ground.

During the anarchy, a sly smuggler had slipped into the weapons building to grab some ammo. Unnoticed by the agents locked in battle, he carried a box of artillery ammo and started restocking the gun. In an instant, the smugglers were dominant as the agents ran for their lives. The helicopters that had previously been barraging the airstrip with their cannons were a target once again as pilots fled from their smoking vehicles.

The agents storming through the weapons building were slowed down on their raid as the almost impenetrable metal doors were automatically locked. It took a extensive amount of firepower to dent a single door and ISIO was facing a losing battle. More of the riflemen were forced to join the skirmishes taking place below them in the building as the agents were overwhelmed.

In the cover of the clouds, Tom felt useless as everyone was bravely battling below him. But he had noticed the artillery gun back in action and he knew he would have to do something about it otherwise someone would get hurt. Earlier, Hawk had fired a missile at the Chinook and Tom remembered exactly which one it was. Without warning, he leapt forward into the cockpit, alarming the pilot who realised what he was doing a second too late. Tom slammed a fist down on the red button, launching the air-to-ground missile.

"Tom! No!" Shouted Hawk as the missile was sent soaring forward. Hawk ran forward to stop Tom but it was too late. The missile had not hit Tom's intended target, the artillery gun. Instead, it crashed into the weapons building. A corner of the building was engulfed in flame. Pieces of concrete and brick came raining down, smashing into tiny fragments as they hit the ground. A larger piece, completely by fluke, hurtled into the artillery gun. The smuggler manning it just had time to jump out of the way before it was demolished. The helicopters struggling to stay in the air regained control as the deadly weapon was destroyed.

Tom was horrified. Hawk was as well, frozen in shock. Tom couldn't tell whether he was angry or happy that he had fired the missile. Either way, it had eliminated a big threat. And gave away their position.

Chapter 21

The attention of the smugglers turned to the clouds. Each and every one of them had seen the missile come out of nowhere. There was something in the clouds. And there were more missiles coming. Seconds after the missile made impact, the Blackhawk and the three people inside it was caught in a hail of bullets. The invading agents weren't their target. The mark was the Blackhawk.

"Not this again!" Hawk yelled as the Blackhawk shuddered. It had already started smoking and now they were in some real danger. The glass of the cockpit had been smashed, making the pilot back away hastily from the jagged glass all over the controls. The helicopter angled forward and Tom found out that there was no ground under his feet and was falling. He managed to grab onto a parachute that had been attached to a coat hanger. If he let go, he would fall through the gap created when the windscreen had been smashed. Wind was whirling around him and Tom couldn't even scream. Tom's grip on the parachute was slipping.

Hawk bounded forwards and grabbed hold of Tom's hand as the parachute was wrenched from the hanger. It was now dangling below him, Hawk holding onto Tom's free hand. "Let go of the parachute!" Hawk shouted into Tom's ear. But Tom had become an expert on life-or-death situations. With a grin, he shouted, "Sorry, Hawk!" before letting go. Tom had a moment to register the look of horror on the man's face before he was falling to his end.

He wasn't even wearing the parachute. Tom hugged it with one hand while scrambling to pull the ripcord. Tom's hand closed around it and he yanked it. The parachute opened and Tom was safe for a second, peacefully floating. Then the smugglers spotted him. Orange flickers whizzed past him but Tom was trapped. He started to descend much quicker and realised the parachute had been pierced by one of the bullets.

Tom shouted in alarm as he started falling. The parachute was only making him fall faster and he ditched it, spreading his arms and legs out to slow down his fall. Like the other agents whose parachutes had been shot down, Tom didn't have far to fall. By the looks of it, he was going to miss the roof of the building and plummet straight into the battlefield. Tom had to do something. With Desert Ghost's plan in mind, he aimed to land in the roof where he could safely get into the building.

It was the wind. Tom had just missed the roof. He was clinging onto the edge of the roof, aware of the fire caused by the missile creeping closer to him. Tom swung his legs back and forth, trying to get some momentum before swinging into the building through a crack created by the missile. He landed hard on the glass-covered floor, rolling across it before coming to a standstill.

He brushed the fragments of glass off him before looking around for any smugglers or agents. It was all clear. He tried to get through the metal door but it wouldn't budge. On the other side, Tom heard guns being fired at the door. Agents were trying to break in. But Tom knew it was no use and crept down a short flight of stairs. He had one thing in his mind: his father. They were probably hiding him in the building, if Desert Ghost had ever found Jacob Flashfire in the first place. Tom carefully climbed down the steps, trying to hurry to escape from the fire trailing into the room while also being quiet so nobody would hear him. If any smugglers found him, he would be finished. If any agents found him, he would be taken out of the compound immediately and it would all be over. Either way, he would have to do this solo.

Tom reached an identical metal door that mercifully wasn't locked. Tom pushed it open, running into the room kicking. There was no one there. Tom was at ease as he inspected the room. There was a huge map of the world that took up one side of the room. On it, there were different coloured marks and shapes spread out across the map. There was a red cross on London with a little flame drawn next to it. That was the attack they were carrying out. Tom saw many others and thought to click a picture of them to show Ms Challaby later but then he remembered his phone was in the rucksack he had left behind in Amastan's village.

Tom left the room and came into a second, larger room where there was an armoury. It had just about any weapon Desert Ghost would need. It was an early Christmas for any soldier. Tom was about to continue into the next room but froze at the sound of footsteps. He threw himself behind a rack full of rifles as the smuggler entered the room. Tom thought he would some ammo and then leave but he ignored the array of weapons and strode towards the rifle rack.

Tom couldn't see his face but he was a wiry, agile man who looked like he wouldn't hesitate to hurt Tom. He had to act fast. As the man was coming closer, Tom stood up and lugged the rack across the floor. The guns fell off, making it lighter and easier to wield. The man was caught off guard and couldn't stop Tom's attack. Tom slammed the rack into the man who was thrown across the room. Tom dropped the rack and started running. He had distracted him for a second but he had given away his position a second time.

He heard a roar of anger from behind him and picked up his pace. Tom slammed the door shut behind him and leapt down the stairs, throwing himself down them in seconds. But it was a dead end. There was a single metal door being guarded by a smuggler. Tom was trapped. But the smuggler was facing the other way and Tom crept up to him, tapping him on the back. He turned around and that was when Tom unleashed a roundhouse kick, pushing his heel into the man's chest. He crumpled to the floor. But against the tough smugglers, he had only brought a couple extra minutes of time as his vicious attacks just didn't have enough power to stop the men.

Tom saw a keycard hanging from the man's belt and he pinched it, swiping the door to unlock it. He jumped inside and shut it, locking it again. He was in a bare room with no ornaments or furniture. There was a chair in the middle of the room. And tied to his was Jacob Flashfire, his father.

"Dad!" Tom ran forwards to greet his father. "What happened to you? You're alright!" A rush of words came out of Tom's mouth. He had found his dad! Jacob was wearing tattered clothes, covered in sand and dirt and he had a large bruise on the side of his face. Other than that, the man was in perfect condition. "Tom!" Jacob reached forward to embrace his sun but was restrained by the handcuffs around his wrists. "Oh no! Where's the key?" Tom asked, frantically looking around. Jacob indicated to a rusty hook by the door which Tom hadn't seen when he entered the room.

"They left it there to tease me since I couldn't get it, being handcuffed to this chair. What are you doing here? I can't believe you found me!" Again, father and son exchanged a babble of words to express their happiness. Tom darted over to the hook and grabbed the small metal key. "That was a bit silly of them, wasn't it?" He went over to his father and unlocked the handcuffs chaining his wrists and legs to the chair. The moment he was free, Jacob hugged his son. But there wasn't any time. The smuggler Tom had met in the weapons room was right outside the door.

"I'll handle this one, son." Jacob took the keycard from Tom and unlocked the door. Seeing him, the smuggler lunged forward but Jacob ducked to the side. He had seen something on the guard still lying on the floor. A torch. Jacob flicked the button and shone the intense light into the smuggler's eyes, blinding him but not for long. "Come on!" he shouted to Tom. The pair ran through the narrow corridor and the battle was right outside, alive once again.

"We're getting out of here. Hey, look." Jacob pointed at the bow and arrow lying against the wall outside another locked door. "That must be part of the assault course the fire-fighters took part in. No one has touched it ever since." Tom saw the potent in the weapon and took it with him, stuffing the singular arrow into his pocket. It was strange running into such an ancient weapon in a modern place like this.

Jacob and Tom burst out through the door. "No!" Tom shouted. The wine tanks had been attached to all the planes and helicopters and they were ready to fly. Tom noticed a lot more smugglers in the battle and realised more had arrived. "They're going to take off!" Tom shouted. Jacob shouted a warning to Tom as a grenade sailed through the air, exploding above them. Tom slid across the floor, narrowly dodging the cascading bricks. They piled on top of each other, blocking off Jacob's escape route. "Dad!" Tom shouted. From behind the pile of rubble, he heard a muffled voice. "I'm fine! You go on without me!"

Tom knew there was no chance of freeing his dad now. The bricks were too heavy to move. Tom raced through the airstrip, his eyes set on the line of aerial vehicles ready to take off. He had to save London. Out of the corner of his eye, he saw a familiar face racing alongside him. His heart sank. It was Bulk. Grinning maliciously, Bulk raced past

Tom. He was faster, stronger. Tom sprinted as fast as he could behind him. His lungs were bursting but he was gaining on the boss of the smugglers. But then, Bulk played a deadly move.

He dodged to the side, sticking out his leg and at full speed, Tom tripped over his leg, flying meters across the ground before crashing into the tarmac painfully. Bulk cackled and ran towards the helicopter that was ready to take off, its rotors spinning. Tom's had landed on his side, his shoulder smashing into the ground. He was pretty sure it was broken but he had bigger problems. The helicopter Bulk was taking had departed, and was slowly going higher and higher. It would only be a matter of time before the rest left as well. He had to stop Bulk.

The bow and arrow. Tom dug it out of his pocket and reached out to the bow lying close to him. Feeling bullets pass overhead, Tom crouched down low. His right shoulder was in pain and he didn't know if he could make the shot. He loaded the bow, before dropping it. His shoulder was too weak to pull it back. Why was it not his left shoulder that had to break?

Tom gritted his teeth and tried again. This time, he was able to get the arrow far enough back to give it some real power. Tom thought back to when he was practising with the bow in his garden, firing at the dummy. It had seemed a thousand years had passed since even though in reality it was only a few days ago. Focus. Clear your mind of any distractions. "Without forgetting the world around you, training your mind to focus at the target, you will not succeed." The words of advice his father had given him bounded around inside his head. Tom had never done anything this big. The fate of an entire city lay in his hands. *It's now or never,* Tom thought as he released the arrow.

Everything came to a standstill. Every eye in the compound was watching the arrow as it soared through the air. The look of horror on Bulk's face as the arrow flew towards the helicopter. Every smuggler watching as millions of pound of money was lost. The agents willing the arrow on, to achieve its goals. Jacob Flashfire watched from a tiny crack in the rubble as his son's arrow hit the bullseye.

Epilogue

Tom was sitting next to Hawk and his father on the row of chairs. The other agents filled the space quickly, coming to attention as Ms Challaby took the stage. She was dressed in a smart lime cardigan with a white buttoned shirt. She wore shiny black shoes on her feet and charcoal trousers. She looked like a businesswoman. Ms. Challaby was holding a mike. She started speaking. "Welcome, agents of ISIO. I'm known for deadly boring speeches so I'm going to move on quickly. I just want to say thank you ever so much for what you've done. We had to deploy every single one of you for our biggest mission yet and you succeeded! We have our beloved Jacob, Desert Ghost has been put to a stop and their leader has been arrested, along with many more. A happy ending, I would say. Don't forget to say thanks to somebody who made the biggest impact on our mission. We couldn't have succeeded without him. That person is Tom."

Tom stood up and beamed as everyone clapped. Hawk and his father were smiling proudly, also clapping. It had been a week since Tom had gotten out of the Sahara. The events after he hit the tank wrapped up the adventure. His arrow had managed to hit the tank attached to the helicopter Bulk was flying away on. The tank had shattered and the wine had spurted out everywhere. Then, the fire that had been raging had set it alight and suddenly there was more fire.

Bulk realised he had lost the tanks so he tried to escape. But the ISIO agents, taking advantage of the confusion, had shot down the helicopter and arrested Bulk. The few remaining helicopters evacuated everyone from the burning airstrip and they were flown back home. It was Desert Ghost's final operation.

Many smugglers had escaped but ISIO were working tirelessly to find them. Each day, dozens of them were captured and Tom was sure that it wouldn't be long until they would all be in prison. After his adventure, Tom was looking forward to rest of the holidays. All he wanted for Christmas was some rest and relaxation (and the latest addition to his favourite video game series). When Tom had arrived back in London, he had been greeted by his mother who was in tears, endlessly happy to have him back but also livid that he had disobeyed her. But her happiness outweighed her anger and everything was back to normal. The family had been reunited and that was that. Tom had saved all of London and put a stop to a mass smuggling operation. Following was a long holiday full of fun, festivities and relaxation.

Tom walked outside, his boots crunching on the gravel outside the building after the short meeting had ended. The sun was setting and Tom could hear the distant honk of horns and people as they tried to get home. Next to him, Hawk was watching the sunset, his eyes fixed on the skyline. "That was one big adventure." he said. Tom smiled."All I hope is that I'll never have to go back to that place." Tom gazed up at the majestic sun as it lit the whole universe and beyond.

THE END

About the Author

Abir is a young author and lives in England. His love for writing started from a young age and he is an avid reader and never took it as a task but classes it as something that relaxes him!

He was the head boy of his primary school and recently started grammar school. He has recently graded to black belt in Martial Art. His books can be enjoyed by young readers and adults.

He inherited his writing genes from his maternal grandmother who is a writer herself.

He is a scout and has been associated with it for more than 7 years. He is a fun loving young boy, liked and loved by his teachers and friends. Abir is a Lego fan, enjoys video games. He is a foodie at heart and is never behind from trying new dishes. Abir is deeply attached to his parents and younger brother who always encourages and supports him to follow his dreams.

Website: www.abirgupta.co.uk